➤Tomahawk – Claim ➤

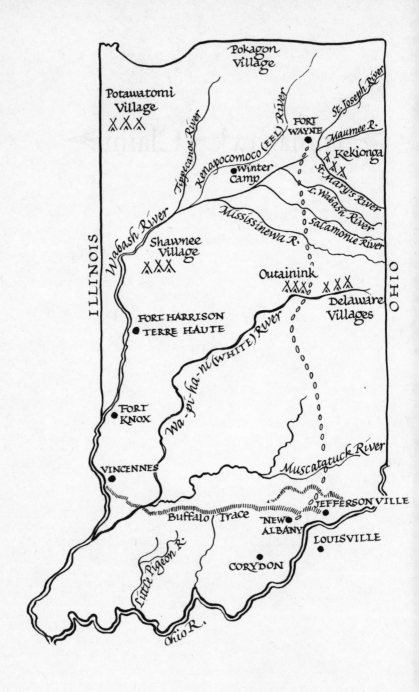

TOMAHAWK

→

CLAIM

Dorothea J. Snow

The BOBBS-MERRILL Company, Inc.
A Subsidiary of Howard W. Sams & Co., Inc.
Publishers   INDIANAPOLIS · KANSAS CITY · NEW YORK

To my own brothers, Bill, Dick, and Ted,
for the wonderful affection we shared.

➤Chapter-1➤

Sixteen-year-old Jonathan Roberts scowled angrily as he stalked out the rear door of the Green Tree Tavern. "That dratted Dave," he muttered, head bent against the wind that whistled over the knobs. "He makes my blood boil."

His brother's mocking laugh rang in his ears as he strode on, shivering. The icy dampness of the raw November day reached to his very bones, it seemed like. A shirt of nettle-bark would have warmed him as much as the fringed shirt he had crawled into that morning, and the buckskin breeches felt as clammy as fish against his flesh.

As loath to leave the snug cabin as was his brother Dave, Jonathan nevertheless was out and on his way. The day's work had to be done, and he was the only one to do it. Resentment rose chokingly within him. If he were free to do as he wanted he could make the troubles of every member of his family vanish like a puff of smoke!

> *John Martin will give liberal prices for bear skins, gray fox, red fox, mink, musk-rat, otter, raccoon, and rabbit. Also beeswax.*

The notice, tucked in a corner of a page of last week's *Corydon Gazette*, flashed through his mind. Oh, he could get good prices for furs, all right—all the money they needed, and in plenty of time, too—if he could only go out and get them. Instead, he had to—— His shoulders shook with anger. . . . That dratted Dave, with his shrugs and grins and flighty ways. . . . Try to talk some sense into him, and like as not he'd start humming or singing one of those silly songs of his.

Raising his head, Jonathan peered through the mists that swirled off the river and cut off his view of the knobs that rose not far behind the tavern he called home.

Then he saw them—the team of oxen and the three men—appear wraithlike from the forest that ringed the clearing. The sight only added fuel to the flames of his anger. Turning abruptly, he went back to the cabin, opened the door, and stuck his head inside.

"They're here, Dave," he snapped. "Make haste, will you?"

Dave's blue eyes regarded him coolly. Sweeping back a lock of long tow-colored hair, he replied, "Keep your shirt on; them logs ain't goin' to run away." Deliberately he scraped the last bit of Indian porridge from the bowl before him, downed the last of his noggin of milk, and wiped the half-moon from his upper lip.

Jon glared at Dave seated at the trestle table, then at the roaring fire in the stone fireplace beyond. Jon, too, liked being warm and taking his time with his victuals. Only he never had the chance to pleasure himself, like Dave. Fury ripped through him.

"They're not going to *move* themselves either," he rasped. "So get out here and lend a hand, will you?"

Dave forced a yawn, rose, and stretched. "Now don't go

8

gettin' riled up." He chuckled. "I'll be there when I get there."

Jon snorted like a winded buffalo. He looked past Dave to the spare figure of his mother busying herself about the hearth.

"Ma," he demanded, "whyn't you slap his sassy mouth?"

She never had and never would; he knew that. She always favored Dave; never made him do anything. Well, it was about time somebody pounded some sense into that addle-pated boy.

Mrs. Roberts straightened up from stirring the contents of the iron kettle that swung on a crane over the fire. "No field is going to get cleared," she said wearily, "long as you two stand there fighting like a couple of roosters."

The words were aimed at Jonathan as well as Dave. Jon could hardly believe it. Couldn't she see that it was Dave who stood in the way of Jon's going north to trap and trade for furs? Furs that would bring in the money they needed to pay the entrance fee on their land?

With a work-worn hand she swept back a wisp of graying hair that had strayed from the tight bun on top of her head. Mrs. Roberts, a tall gaunt woman with deep lines in her weathered face, said softly, "Now, get along, both of you."

Jon's anger melted into contrition. Ma had enough troubles without his adding to them. He knew she was blaming him right now for the morning's quarrel with Dave. He supposed it would be better if he could just swallow his anger at his brother and turn the other cheek, as the Good Book told him to do. He wished he could tell Ma right now that he was really trying to lift her burden rather than—but he wasn't as glib as Dave.

Just look at Dave now, bowing and squeaking, "Anything you say, my lady."

But it had the right effect. Ma's mouth twitched, and she came as close to a smile as she could manage these days. Dave and his silly ways could do it every time. It wasn't all bad, though, Jon had to admit.

Not to be outdone this morning, he gave a loud sniff and pointed to the kettle. "Mean for them to eat well, don't you, Ma?" Such banter came hard to him. Ma sensed its purpose and rose to the occasion.

"That's what they come for," she said. "Even if they do get the same vittles they get at home."

Jon pressed his advantage. "But they're not getting the same," he insisted. "Same things may go in the pot, but they don't come out tasting the same."

Dave looked surprised at such chatter from his usually glum brother. He wasn't about to be outdone either.

"Ma could cook a mess of chickweed," he said loudly, "and make it taste like sweet 'tater pudding."

Ma almost laughed. Why did Dave always have to best him at this too? Jon wondered.

"Oh, go on, you two," Ma said, pleased. "Sound just like your pa."

"What's wrong with that?"

The voice from the doorway to the dogtrot also sounded pleased, but the cheer in it was forced, both Ma and the boys knew. They winced as they watched the tall thin man, his shock of hair almost white, limp painfully into the room and settle, grimacing, into the splint-bottomed chair in front of the fire.

Thomas Roberts was a mockery of the man who three and one half years before had brought his family into the wild free reaches of the Indiana Territory and hacked out the boundary of his land claim with his hunting knife.

10

"It won't be a tomahawk claim for long," he'd said then, using the expression coined by the settlers for those parcels of land so marked; and he'd set to work building the cabin. "I'll build me a sawmill right here on this creek and saw and sell lumber. That'll bring in enough to pay the entrance fee, and then I can have it registered at the land office, right and proper."

So far as land was concerned, Pa hadn't been greedy. He'd marked off roughly 320 acres, half a section as the government would survey it. And $320 would pay for it. One fourth of that—$80—would register it in Thomas Roberts' name at the land office.

Pa had swung Ma into the air then, and she'd laughed happily. Ma could smile in those days, as bright and pretty as any girl, Jon recalled.

"It will take three more payments, like size," she'd reminded him breathlessly, "to pay for it in full."

Her husband had waved a carefree hand. "That'll be easy!" he'd cried. "Settlers'll be pouring in here now the Indian trouble is over; folks from back east with money, not from Kaintuck without a copper, like we were. They'll want sawed lumber houses, and the man here first with a sawmill will get rich. Likely before long I'll be taking up more land."

Always the practical one, Ma had put first things first. "Let's pay for this land before we start buying more." But her eyes had shone with pleasure.

Then shortly afterward had come the War of 1812. Impressment of American seamen into the British navy had stirred the ire of the folks back east. On the frontier, it was the Indians the settlers were worried about. With the British backing them, the Indians attacked with a ferocity they had never shown before.

To meet that danger, Thomas Roberts and hundreds of others like him had marched north from their homes on the Ohio.

Her husband had no sooner disappeared into the woods than Mrs. Roberts turned to her children. "We'll pay the entrance fee and keep the land and cabin for your pa to come back to," she'd told them, struggling to keep her real fears hidden. "He can build his sawmill then."

"How we going to do that, Ma?" Jon, not yet fourteen, had asked.

"We're going to turn this fine double cabin into a tavern," his mother had replied. "Travelers will be coming through and stopping."

She had made covers for cornshuck mattresses, which she then laid on the floors of the sleeping rooms across the dog-trot. Every day she saw to it that the cooking pot was full of tasty rabbit or squirrel stew and that there was plenty of fresh cornbread baked on the hearth. And she scrubbed and scoured and kept the place cleaner than most.

She depended mainly on Jon, her eldest. Jon hunted and brought home the stew meat. He didn't complain, for hunting was what he liked to do most. But he did have trouble with Dave. It took prodding to get his younger brother to plant and hoe the small patch of cleared land, to carry water from the nearby spring, and to curry and feed the travelers' horses.

Folks did stop—post riders carrying mail between Louis-ville and Vincennes, and occasional straggling settlers. Ma carefully hoarded the cash she took in, hoping to have the entrance fee on the land paid when Pa got back.

But the growing fear that the Indians would swoop down from the forests around the northern forts soon slowed the flow of travelers to a trickle. Ma was far short of the $80 entrance fee by the time her husband returned.

So Pa came back to the same tomahawk claim he had left. To make matters worse, his health was shattered. Two Indian arrows had found their mark, and rheumatism and ague now plagued him.

"Better I was dead than a burden to my family," he said bitterly when comrades, not much better off than Pa himself, had brought him home.

"You'll be well and strong again in no time," his wife assured him as confidently as her aching heart would allow.

She gave him every potion or tonic anyone suggested. Dave spent most of his time hunting roots and herbs in the woods and along the creek bank. Emma, under Ma's watchful eye, then boiled them into evil-smelling liquids to be poured into him, or, when mixed with bear grease, to be rubbed on him.

Patiently Pa swallowed them and let them be smeared on his chest and joints. He choked down Ma's good food, though he felt little hunger. Nothing seemed to help. Some days he seemed better, some days worse. . . .

Now it was late fall of 1815, and the war had been over almost a year.

Emma bustled into the room. "The Simonses and Barkuses are here," she announced.

Jon shot a glance of approval at his fifteen-year-old sister. She knew what the arrival of two more of their neighbors that morning meant to him. But then she'd always shown more sense and gumption than Dave.

Emma began clearing the table, taking off the bowl and noggin that Dave had just used. Her gaze met Jon's. If she

13

had her way, the look implied, she'd make Dave get out earlier in the morning.

Jon leveled a stern look at Dave. "That don't surprise me. Lots of folks get out and doing before time for noonday meal."

Dave glared back. "Aw, shut your jawing," he growled. Half angry himself now, Dave jerked a fringed shirt from a peg on the wall by the door. He pulled it on over his tousled hair and linsey-woolsey undershirt and followed Jon outside, mimicking his older brother's purposeful stride.

Uriah let out a whoop of laughter, and Jon knew Dave was up to some of his foolishness. But he never looked back.

"You'd best get a hustle on today," he said in his best no-nonsense manner. "This field's got to be cleared before night." He lifted his head and sniffed. "It's coming on to snow; I can smell it."

At a half lope Dave tried to keep up with Jonathan.

"You can smell it!" He chuckled derisively and wagged his head until the tail of his coonskin cap slapped first one cheek, then the other. "Pity you weren't born an Indian, you try so hard to be one."

Jon ignored the remark. "I can always tell when it's coming on to rain or snow," he said proudly. "It's in the air, and I can smell it, same as an Indian can."

Dave took an extra long lope and came up even with his brother.

"More of Old Josh's wood learning," he jeered. An impish gleam came into his blue eyes. "I can tell it's likely to snow too," he said. "And I don't lay no claim to being a Dan'l Boone. But those clouds are snow clouds, and besides it's coooold."

Jon stalked on. Let Dave make light of everything; he'd

14

soon find out that being the head of a family was no funning matter.

Jon's eyes took in the felled trees that lay every which way. Dave had helped girdle and fell the trees and cut them into lengths that could be snaked out with a team, though his singing and humming had tried Jon's patience.

"You're thirteen years old, Dave," he had told him. "It's high time you grew up."

Dave's eyes had twinkled. "Are you grown up?"

"I sure am."

"Then I don't ever want to be, if it means being a sour pill like you."

"Well, just you wait . . ." Jon had started to tell Dave his plans, then had buttoned his lips and gone back to chopping.

Trees felled and ready, Jon had passed the word around the settlement along Falling Run Creek that there would be a logrolling at the Roberts place. Today was the day, and if enough neighbors showed up, the field would be cleared of all but stumps by nightfall.

"Got to be careful not to break a share plowing 'round these stumps," he told Dave now.

Dave turned serious for once. "If you had your heart set on farming, Jon," he said slowly, "instead of hunting and trapping, a little thing like plowing around stumps wouldn't fret you much."

Jon was at a loss for words. Dave was right, and Jon knew it. He hated plowing and planting and hoeing and being pinned down to a patch of ground. Tramping through the forests, rifle on shoulder, was more to his liking. He'd be glad when Dave could take over all such tasks about the home place.

Why not now? He was old enough!

15

"I'm going to talk to Ma this very night," Jon muttered resolutely.

Dave turned to look at him. "What you jawing about now?"

"Aw, shet up!"

➤Chapter-2

"Mornin', Mr. Simons," Jon respectfully greeted the slight, sandy-haired man standing beside a fine team of oxen. "Mighty nice of you to come."

Simon squinted. "The Lord was willing," was his thin-lipped reply.

A hard-rock Baptist, John Simons worshipped a tyrant God. Life on earth to him was a grim mission, a test trial for the life beyond the grave.

"Man born to woman," he said often, rolling his pale eyes heavenward, "is born to trouble all his days." With uncommon zeal he screened off from his own life and that of his family any pleasures there might be.

Though respected by his neighbors for both his honesty and his capacity for hard work, he was feared by his wife and children. One small slip from any of them could subject all of them—guilty and innocent alike—to a fiery tongue lashing better suited to the vilest of sinners.

Jon despised the man. It was hard even now to be polite to him. But he did manage a friendly grin at Luke and Sam, the

Simons boys, standing beside their father. They were big burly fellows, each capable of lifting his father with one hand. Yet they obeyed his every command as meekly as the dog that sat on its haunches between them.

"Howdy, Luke," Jon said warmly, for the Simons boys, though shy as rabbits, were as likable as their father was not. "Howdy, Sam."

The boys were bears for work too. With them helping, the trees would disappear from the field as fast as a bowl of Ma's stew before a hungry traveler.

"Howdy, Jon," Luke and Sam replied in unison, as they did almost everything. Then reddening as usual at the slightest recognition, they shut up like frightened clams.

The elder Simons did the talking for his family. "How's yer pa?" he asked sternly, as though Jon were responsible for his father's condition.

Bridling at the man's attitude, Jon forced a "Poorly."

Rubbing folks' fur the wrong way was another of John Simons' traits. "It's the Lord's will," he said piously.

"Amen." Mrs. Simons, in her thin, piping voice, backed up her husband.

Jon and Dave turned to see her slide from the back of the tired-looking horse she had ridden over. Two small, skinny girls—Lory and Cory—slid like little ghosts after her. Jon caught the look of expectant eagerness on the pinched face of their mother as she hurried toward the Robertses' cabin.

Who could blame her? An opportunity like this, sharing small talk with neighbor women, came to her seldom. Away from her grim husband she had even been seen to smile on occasion.

"Mornin', Katie Mae," Jon greeted the last of the Simons

18

family to appear. He tried to be offhand about it, knowing every eye was upon him. Dave's particularly had an impish gleam.

Just why anybody should think he was interested in that thin little thing beneath the floppy sunbonnet, Jon would never know. He guessed it was because he was a young man and she a young woman of fifteen, and that they were neighbors and sometimes spoke to each other.

"Mornin', Jon," she answered so faintly she could scarcely be heard. Shoulders hunched, and hands clutching a basket of food, she hurried after her mother, aware that her father's watery eyes were watching her with suspicion.

Jon's anger, never far below the surface, almost flared into view. It was with real effort that he held back from telling the evil-minded old man just what he thought of him. But it wouldn't do. The man would always see something sinful between his daughter and every fellow who spoke to her. Besides, he needed the help of the Simons boys and those oxen to clear the field.

"Simons puts his trust in the Lord," Jon's father had once remarked, adding dryly, "and He is about the only one Simons does trust."

Katie Mae, Jon knew, moved in holy fear of her father ever since he'd caught her tapping a foot to the lively tune of a fiddler at a neighborhood hoedown.

In an undertone, Dave said, "He'd give a body the itching fidgets." Then he yelled suddenly, "Here come the Barkuses!" and was off like a shot. Off to greet the youngest of the Barkus family, Jack, a boy about Dave's age. Jon would have to keep an eye on them, fun-loving as they were. Barkus didn't have the control over his boys that Simons did, a fact that didn't seem to bother the big, red-headed man who strode toward them now.

"Powerful glad to see you!" Jon cried, and meant it, as he welcomed Les Barkus and his strapping son Mark.

"Mighty glad to help you out," Barkus boomed. He winked plainly. "And we'll welcome the tasty vittles and the fiddling afterward, too."

Simons motioned sternly to Luke and Sam to get to work on the logs. The noisy, pleasure-loving Barkuses were not to his liking, and he made no effort to hide his feelings.

If the Barkuses cared they didn't show it.

"Missus come?" Jon asked, eyeing Dave and Jack cavorting like a couple of puppies not far away.

Barkus pushed back his battered old skin cap and scratched the head beneath it. "Nope. Said she weren't feeling so pert this morning."

"Too bad," Jon said, though he wasn't surprised. Mrs. Barkus rarely felt well.

"The pining sickness is what ails her," Jon's mother had said knowingly. "Lots of women get that in the wilderness. Can't stop pining for the homes they left behind and their loved ones back there."

Ma was like that, Jon thought, always feeling sorry for others. The neighbors liked her, though they thought her peculiar in some ways.

Barkus' keen blue eyes squinted about at the felled trees, oak, maple, hackberry, and sycamore. "Ain't it a fright," he said, "how these pesky things grow so thick? Where'll we start?"

"Just about anywhere." Jon pointed to the edge of the field of felled trees. "Aimin' to pile them over there and have a sky fire come evening."

"Then we'd best start over there," Barkus said briskly, "and work our way back."

Jon saw the sense to that, and nodded.

Barkus turned to his middle son. "C'mon, Mark, with them spikes."

Mark quickly fetched two huge iron spikes, and he and his father set to work. Mark held a spike while his father tapped it lightly to set it into the big end of a tree trunk. Then, swinging their heavy mallets in rhythm, each striking the head of the spike in turn, they drove it deep into the wood. When both spikes were in, chains were wrapped around them and fastened to the whiffletree of the harness hitched to the yoke of oxen.

Barkus handed the rein to his youngest son. "You, Jack."

Jack took the rein and led the heavy-footed, powerful animals to the edge of the field. The log snaked along behind. Dave ran alongside the log and when it was where they wanted it, he loosened the spikes with a sledge hammer.

Dave can work, Jon thought, when he wants to.

"How's yer pa?" Barkus asked as they waited for the return of spikes and team.

"Sometimes it seems like he's better, and again seems like he's backslid," Jon replied.

A look of concern flicked over Barkus' kindly face. For two long years he and Jon's father had fought side by side. He had helped bring Thomas Roberts back. He spat. "Paid yer entrance fee yet?"

Jon shook his head slowly.

"Too bad," Barkus went on. "I've been hearin' that land-grabbers will soon be busy buying up land hereabouts. Gov-'ment in Washington needs the money and don't seem to care if they sell it right out from under folks that fought the

Indians, the folks who have every right to it even though they don't have the cash to get their claims registered at the land office."

"Yeah, I know." Jon's voice was bitter. Nobody knew better than he that a tomahawk claim was no claim at all, as far as the land office was concerned.

Barkus' voice turned bitter then. "Grabbers don't want to live on the land. They jest want to hold it till they can git a sight more than they paid for it." He waved his hand about. "Now the Injuns been beat, folks from back east will be glad to pay their prices."

Jon's face hardened. "They won't get our land," he said fiercely. "Come spring, and I'll have that eighty-dollar fee." He looked up at the darkening sky. "Nobody's likely to come into this wilderness this time of year, so I'm safe till then."

He had his plans laid. All he had to do was talk to Ma. Just get her to see that Dave took on his responsibility for caring for the family's needs this coming winter. That would leave him free to go north with Old Josh to trap and trade for furs.

Animals had been pretty well thinned out about the knobs here. Up north was where they were thick in the woods and streams. Prime pelts he'd bring back after a winter up there around Fort Wayne, bundles and bundles of them. They'd bring enough to pay the fee and then some, maybe even enough to make the other three payments. That would leave their land free and clear.

A shiver of pure delight went through him at the very thought. The family'd look up to him then, all right. And Dave would be put in his proper place in Ma's eyes.

Ma! He hadn't even mentioned his plan to her yet. Would she be willing to spend the winter without an able-bodied man around the place?

If only Dave would grow up! Disgustedly he thought of that great big young 'un who had just last evening spent the whole time making a cornstalk fiddle for Uriah!

> *Go tell Aunt Rhody,*
> *Go tell Aunt Rhody,*
> *Go tell Aunt Rhody,*
> *The old gray goose is dead!*

Over and over the two had sung that flighty song until Jon, thoroughly peeved, had gone up the ladder to bed.

Dave and Jack returned with the team and spikes, and Barkus and Mark started on another log. Jon felt better.

A lot depended on clearing this field today. He could go north with Old Josh with a clear conscience. Dave could plow and plant it before Jon came back in the spring.

The Lyonses, neighbors from along the creek, arrived then. As they brought neither horses nor oxen, Jon set them to piling the logs and brush so they would burn well. But first he asked, "Bring your fiddle, Doug?"

Doug Lyons was tall and lanky and homely as a mud fence, as everybody agreed, but he was popular and more than welcome at neighborhood bees and logrollings. After a long day of work his rollicking tunes could banish fatigue and set everybody to dancing.

Jon had made sure the Simonses were out of earshot before asking. No sense making them mad before they'd done any work.

Doug's eyes followed in the direction of Jon's gaze. He replied in a voice edged with scorn, "Didn't think a bunch o' shoutin' Baptists'd make me leave it home, did you?"

"Now, Doug, it ain't right to talk about your neighbors

so," plump Mrs. Lyons reproved. "Everybody to his own notion."

"And I got a right to mine," Doug replied, a sheepish grin creeping across his thin, pock-marked features. He handed his fiddle to his mother. "Take good care of it."

"Don't fret." His mother smiled. "It's as dear to me as to you, for it was my own pa brought it from across the sea years ago."

"I'd give my right arm for one as good as that," Dave said.

"No, you wouldn't," said Mrs. Lyons, "for without an arm how could you fiddle?"

"With my toes," Dave shot back good-humoredly.

I could whack him, Jon thought; always smarting off.

Ed Lyons, a tall wizened man with wispy gray hair, spoke up as his wife and three tiny daughters, Ruth, Effie, and Pearl, started toward the cabin, "Best I cut and pile?"

Jon nodded, and he and Lyons and Doug walked to the spot where four logs were now stacked, along with branches and saplings that the Simonses had piled alongside. Using axes, they began getting the logs in better shape to burn.

As they worked, Ed Lyons said, "New family built a lean-to up the creek a ways from our place. Three young 'uns and a man. Woman's dead, I reckon, and man's ailing." He shook his head. "Don't see how they aim to make out this winter. Come too late to clear any land, or plant, or build a proper shelter even."

"They'll have to get along same as others," John Simons spoke up. "Lord helps those that help theirselves."

Ed Lyons ignored the Biblical admonition and continued. "Name's Liddicoat, I found out. Girl's about fifteen years old. Young feller's older but mighty puny-looking. Least one's about Uriah's age."

24

"They need help," Doug said, stopping to toss a branch on the ever-growing pile. "Our help." And he shot a look at Simons.

Lyons frowned at his son. "I've took them a poke of meal," he said.

Jon knew what was expected of him. "I'm going hunting soon," he said. "I'll leave them some meat."

Lyons seemed satisfied.

Other neighbors came—the Johnsons, then the Mitchells. There were two more men and two women, as well as several boys and girls.

The work went on all morning. The air grew increasingly raw and cold and the sky threatened snow. In spite of the work being done, Jon's anxiety grew by the hour.

Would they get the field cleared before the storm struck? If not, it might be days before they could get back to it. By that time Old Josh would be on his way up north.

➤Chapter-3➤

Young Billy Johnson, the three Lyons girls, and the two little Mitchell boys stood shyly, eyes big with longing, staring at the trestle table.

"Won't be nothing left but fat and scrapings time we get to eat." Billy sighed loudly.

Mrs. Roberts had cooked turkey and gravy and corn dumplings, and Mrs. Lyons had brought hog and hominy. There was a big bowl of Injun pudding, and honey to pour over it. All this and squash pie, plum preserves, and buttermilk besides.

Billy watched his father sit on a stool by the hearth beside Mr. Lyons and Mr. Barkus. "Be glad when I'm a man grown and get first lick at the vittles," he piped up.

Ruth Lyons also had her eye on the parade of hungry men. "And I'll be glad," she said, "when I'm a woman grown and get a second chance."

Everybody in the crowded Roberts cabin laughed at this, even the women, who were making sure more food was put on the table as fast as it was taken off.

It was Mrs. Roberts who turned to the children and said

soothingly, "Now don't fret. There'll be plenty left for you to eat."

Uriah, who was standing a bit apart, shot the others his age a triumphant look. Only moments before he had told them, "My ma don't hold with the notion that least ones only get to eat what the grown-ups leave." They hadn't believed him either when he'd added, "I get to eat at the table with them." Maybe now they would, his look implied.

The men had come quickly when the call had gone out that the noon meal was ready. Now, trenchers in hand, they were filing down along the length of the table while the women and children waited their turn.

Jon ate with the rest of the men. Though he wasn't accustomed to eating before his mother or Emma or even Uriah, his mother had told him to do as the others did. His father joined them for the meal, as did Dave, who needed no urging.

When the men had had all the helpings they wanted, the women filled their own trenchers and gathered in a corner by themselves. All except Mrs. Roberts. She put a fresh supply of food on the table and motioned to the children.

"It's just the same as Pa had on his trencher!" Billy gasped as he looked at the turkey and gravy and dumplings she had dished up for him. "Glory be!"

Soon all the youngsters were eating with loud smacking sounds of enjoyment. And they went back for second helpings too.

Jon was proud of his ma. He was glad that in some ways she was different from the other women. But then her father, as Jon had often heard, had been a prosperous gristmill owner. He had even sent her—a girl—to school, and she could read and write. That also set her apart.

When their trenchers were empty the men set them on the

floor and stood up. "If we aim to get that field cleared before it snows, we'd best get back to work," Barkus said. He emitted a loud belch and started for the door. The others, following him, suddenly stopped in their tracks as a loud, bloodcurdling whoop came from outside.

"Injuns!" Mrs. Simons whispered hoarsely.

"It ain't Injuns," Les Barkus snorted; "it's them Larkin hardbats up to more of their devilment." He strode to the door and threw it open. "Cuttin' loose the critters and chasing them off into the woods."

Fury giving wings to his feet, Jon ran past the others and out the door. This mustn't happen now. It could take all day to find animals lost among the trees and bring them home. And the field couldn't be cleared without them.

The men buzzed angrily behind him. "Need the livin' lard beat out of them, them Larkins do," one said.

Jon agreed. The Larkins were always stealing, breaking up camp meetings, running off cattle, raising cain in general, and folks seemed powerless to do anything about it.

Jon and Dave were beside the Simonses now. Mr. Simons and his sons were watching their team of oxen disappear into the woods with a yelling Larkin in hot pursuit. The other Larkin, they could see, was working furiously to loose the Barkus team.

Luke and Sam were straining at the leash of their anger. But they wouldn't move without their father's say-so.

Well, wouldn't the man ever speak? Jon wondered impatiently.

"An eye for an eye and a tooth for a tooth," Simons said finally, and he nodded to Luke and Sam. "Go git that team any way you can."

The two big fellows were off like twin arrows from a long bow.

Mark raced after the shadowy figure untying the Barkus team. All three were followed by the other men, shouting encouragement.

Jon's eyes swept toward the barnshed. The gate of the sheeppen was open and four sheep were racing toward the woods. The cow was gone too.

"They'll all get lost and freeze to death," he moaned. The thought of such a disaster left him limp. With those animals went the family's warm clothing and much of their winter food supply.

He caught sight then of a slender figure trying to mount Old Lightning. Surprise mingled with his rising fury. This was no Larkin. You couldn't mistake a member of that ill-begotten crew—short and squat, with hands reaching to the knees; flat faces with small eyes set close together.

"They're not running off Old Lightning," he vowed as he ran toward the shed.

Old Lightning wasn't cooperating with his would-be rider. He was shying and prancing and almost living up to the name he had been given years before.

Jon was halfway to the shed when he heard feet pounding behind him. How many were in this Larkin bunch anyhow? Fearfully he turned, expecting someone to leap on him. Instead he saw Dave and Jack following him, looking as determined as Jon felt.

"Go get the sheep and the cow!" he shouted. "They've been run off too." He was grateful to see them swerve and head for the woods, where the haunches of the sheep were almost out of sight.

Reaching the shed, Jon caught a glimpse of a white frightened face and wondered again who the newcomer was. He'll be a lot more scared when I get through with him, he thought grimly.

The stranger managed to fling himself onto the rearing horse's back. Jon made a lunge for one of his legs. Old Lightning shied, and Jon fell flat on his face.

The stranger laughed shrilly. Furious, Jon got to his feet just as the rider goaded the horse into a run. Jon took out after them.

He had to catch them. He couldn't let Old Lightning be left a mile or two in the woods. That would mean a hunt for him, time taken away from clearing the field. From the looks of things there would be enough time lost trying to find the animals already gone.

If I don't have the worst luck! he thought bitterly. All this trouble today of all days. He could picture Old Josh now, on his way north, alone.

What did that flapbrain think he was doing anyway, heading a horse across a field with logs lying all around? Didn't he know a horse could stumble over one and break a leg? And have to be shot? Without a horse the Roberts family would really be in a fix.

Then it happened: Old Lightning stumbled over a limb and went down to his knees. His rider flew right out over his head. The thought of what had happened to the horse was all but forgotten by the exultation Jon felt at seeing the unknown rider sprawl in the brushy part of a tree.

Jon was upon the prostrate form before it had a chance to recover from the shock of falling. He sat firmly astride it and poured out his anger in blows to the head and shoulders beneath him.

The boy—he soon realized it was a boy and a small one at that—breathed heavily. That didn't stop Jon's drubbing fists. "I'm going to beat the stuffing out of you," Jon shouted, "for riding off with our horse and making him break a leg in the bargain."

A feeble gasp came from the slender form, and then it went limp. The face in the dirt, Jon saw, had finely chiseled features and eyelashes an inch long! Just like a girl's face, he thought scornfully. He could beat him with his hands tied. The back beneath him arched and he almost lost his seat!

"Why, you little varmint!" he yelled, his fists going to work again.

He didn't see Luke and Sam round up their team of oxen. Nor did he see the Larkin who had been chasing it flee at sight of them. It wouldn't have surprised him, though. Everybody knew the Larkins were cowards, sneaking around at night and running like rats when cornered.

He didn't see Mark and Doug chase off the other Larkin trying to untie the Barkus team either, or Dave and Jack bring back the sheep and cow. All he could see was the form beneath him and his own fists pounding on it. But the boy didn't holler, he had to admit that.

"Break his neck!" somebody yelled. "Be too good for him."

"Poke his eyes out!" another urged.

Then a shrill cry broke through the raucous yells, so near Jon's ear it seemed to split his eardrum.

"Leave him be!" the voice cried out in terror. "Leave my brother be!"

Jon felt small fists raining blows on his own head and shoulders. The face below him grimaced. "Aw, go away, sis," the words came chokingly. "I can take care of myself."

31

"You're not doing it now, Pike." The fists beat faster and more sharply on Jon's head. "Leave him be!" the girl howled louder in his ear.

Fearing a trick, Jon turned slightly, and saw a small white pinched face, with eyes so big they looked like burned holes in a blanket. And framing them were lashes long and black as smudges. It was a girl, all right, a painfully thin one, wrapped in a ragged piece of what once had been brown homespun. Hardly enough to ward off the icy wind that blew in from the knobs.

Still, it was this brother of hers who had caused him and his family so much trouble. Why should he . . . ?

"I'll let your brother be," Jon said evenly, "if you'll get him out of this field and see to it he never comes back."

As he rose from the still-prostrate figure a groan of disappointment rose from the onlookers.

"And it looked like it'd be a good fight, too," he heard someone say.

Jon shrugged. In some ways he was like his ma—different. He'd never taken any pleasure in fighting or in watching others fight until bones and teeth were broken and eyes gouged out.

The girl was on her knees beside her brother. She slipped a skinny arm beneath his head and cried, "Pike! Pike! Are you hurt? Say something, Pike!"

Jon was drained of any triumph he might have felt. Who were these two, anyway?

"It's the Liddicoats," Ed Lyons said then, coming up beside Jon.

"What are they doing with the Larkins?" John asked; then seeing that Mark was getting Old Lightning to his feet, he called anxiously, "Leg broke?"

"Don't 'pear to be," Mark yelled back.

Relieved, Jon turned to Lyons for the answer to his other question.

With a shake of his head, Lyons replied, "Been wonderin' myself. They don't seem the same stripe at all."

Brother and sister left, arms about each other in such a way it was hard to tell who was supporting whom.

"Old Lightnin' ain't hurt a'tall!" Dave's joyous shout rang out.

Jon's joy was great at sight of the old horse rising and shaking himself as if to find out for himself if all his pieces were intact.

At dusk the field was cleared. "Sky fire, sky fire!" the chant went up as lighted torches were thrown into the piles of brush and logs fringing the field. Shortly the workers would head for the cabin for more food and for the music and dancing that would follow.

"Ain't it a pretty sight?" Katie Mae smiled shyly up at Jon as flames leaped into the blue-black sky.

"It is for certain sure," Jon replied, looking down at her. But instead of Katie Mae's face, he saw a girl with great smudges of eyes, wearing a ragged dress that flapped on her thin form.

➤Chapter-4➤

It was a sight easier to make Ma see things his way than Jon had thought. After the neighbors had left and the rest of the family had gone to bed, he told her of his plan.

"Old Josh says there are prime pelts for the taking up north," Jon said as they sat before the dying flames on the hearth. "Sold for top prices they'll bring more than enough for that entrance fee, come spring."

Ma looked thoughtfully into the fire. "Be careful, son. The Indians up there are still mad as wounded bears. They may seem peaceful now the war is over, but they're not above taking revenge on a white man if the chance offers itself."

He could take care of himself, Jon thought; it was Dave she should fret about. But he covered his annoyance easily, he was that glad he could go. "I'll take care," he promised.

"And I'll take in what folks come by and stop," his mother said, "and save what I can."

"No need for that, Ma, unless you want to," Jon said with confidence. "Furs I bring back will sell for enough money to take care of things."

Ma put her own rough hand over his. "You can't be sure

until you have it in your hand." She smiled. "Just you be careful, that's the main thing."

Love for his mother welled up in Jon, and with it the determination to lighten her load of care. Eighty dollars—why, that wasn't much really. Not with beaver and such just waiting up north for him to trap and trade the Indians for. Once that fee was paid no land-grabber could buy their land out from under them. . . .

Cooking smells were drifting up through the cracks in the floor when he awakened next morning. Jon stirred guiltily beside Dave. Ma was up and about, had stirred the slumbering fire and put on more wood. The Injun pudding was warming on the hearth, and the room below was cozy now, if one didn't get too far from the fire.

Should have got up and fixed the fire myself, Jon thought, twisting so as to give Dave a thump with a hip. He thought gleefully, That'll be Dave's chore this winter.

Still he lay there. It had snowed all night and there was no need to get up too early. Besides, it was so comfortable under the pile of quilts, watching his breath rise in steamy clouds in the cold air of the loft room he shared with Dave and Uriah.

Suddenly an urge seized him. It wasn't often he did such a thing, but right now he couldn't resist the temptation. He let out a loud whoop, jumped up, and dragged the covers with him. Then he stood and grinned down at Dave sputtering sleepily and making a frantic grab for a corner of the covers.

Awake at last, Dave glared up at his brother. "Find a snake in bed?" he snarled.

"For a bit I thought your leg was one," Jon chuckled.

"Right now I wisht it was and it would rare up and bite you good." Dave made another grab for the covers and got a hold of them. Jon let them go and watched Dave fall back with a thump.

Both were shivering now as Jon struggled into his icy buckskins and Dave twisted and turned in an effort to pull the unruly covers over his chest and keep them over his feet at the same time.

"Talk about growing up," he grumbled as he settled back for more sleep. "Seems like you'd better do some yourself."

Jon stopped at the top of the ladder. "Remember wood has to be cut for firewood this winter—lots of it."

One blue eye was all that was visible from under the covers. It was as cold as the air, and so was Dave's voice. "I'm not likely to forget with you around."

The cover muffled a loud exaggerated snoring.

Once down the ladder Jon's feeling of guilt disappeared. It was Emma who was busying herself about the fireplace.

"I knew you'd be going over to Josh's this morning," she said quietly, dishing up a helping of pudding for him, "so I got up to fix you a bite to eat. Ma's sleeping like the dead."

Jon nodded and sat down at the trestle table. Emma must have heard him and Ma talking the night before. She'd guessed he'd waste no time going over to tell his friend he would be going north with him.

"I wish I could go with you," Emma said wistfully.

Jon felt himself swelling up inside. Even Emma realized the importance of his leaving and wanted to take part in his undertaking.

"No place for womenfolk," he said, pouring honey over his pudding.

Emma's wistfulness vanished. "I hate being a girl!" she burst out heatedly.

Jon gulped. Emma was usually so quiet and mouselike,

36

given to taking orders and obeying them. Too bad Dave wasn't more like her; things would go a lot easier.

"No help for that now," Jon said lightly.

He was glad to see Ma come into the room from her and Pa's sleeping quarters across the dogtrot. It made him uncomfortable sometimes, talking to Emma. A woman's lot wasn't easy, staying home and fixing and doing for the comfort of others. He was glad he hadn't been born one.

"Slept later than I figgered on," Ma said, securing her bun of hair with a wooden pin Dave had whittled for her. "But I was tuckered out last night, I tell you."

"No wonder," Jon said, "all the folks you were doing for."

"We got that field cleared though, didn't we?" Ma said, sounding pleased. "And everybody had a good time afterward."

"Everybody but the Simonses," Jon said. "And it pretty near broke Katie Mae's heart when her pa made them all leave soon's Doug got out his fiddle."

Jon had been relieved when they'd gone, though. Katie Mae had made him feel uneasy, looking at him with her sad eyes. Well, he wasn't ready for courting any girl, least of all a Simons.

Ma turned to Emma. "Why didn't you dance?" she asked.

"Nobody asked me." Emma stirred the pudding vigorously, her eyes avoiding theirs.

"Nobody could see you," Jon teased, "hiding behind those pots and pans all evening."

Then he wished he hadn't said it. He knew that Emma had cleared and stacked and washed pots and pans and trenchers on purpose. It would have hurt more to have been in plain sight and have no young man pay her any attention. The older boys had had eyes only for Mitchell's two girls anyway.

37

"Plenty of time to keep company with the cook kettle when you get married," Ma chided Emma. Though she had doubts that it would ever happen. Ma worried about Emma —fifteen years old and no beau in sight.

Emma wasn't pretty. Big and rawboned, her face was flat like Dave's and her mouth too large. But on Dave it looked good. They took after the Roberts side of the family.

Jon was tall and slim, with his mother's dark good looks, or what had been good looks when she'd been young. He never thought much about it though, having seen his reflection only in the piece of shiny metal Pa used for shaving.

Jon finished his pudding and rose to go. "Going over to Josh's," he said, as he slapped his skin hat on his head. "Best get Dave down, Ma, and get him started on that firewood. I'd like to see a big stack of it all cut by the time I leave."

Dave's head appeared in the ladder opening. "Then how about cutting some of it yourself, clapperjaw?" he said.

"Oh, shet up!" Jon stormed out the door. Why Ma didn't set on that boy he'd never know.

Once outside he decided he'd look at his traps first. If there was anything in them, he'd pick it up on his way back. All eight of them were set along the bank of the creek, and that was the way he was going anyhow.

There was nothing in the first three traps. So he trudged around a bend of the creek and toward the spot where he had hidden another one in the snakelike roots of a tree that grew half in and half out of the bank.

The soft new snow came up well over the tops of his moccasins. His feet were soon wet and cold. It was still coming down in soggy flakes, but not so hard he didn't see the slim figure in ragged homespuns run from the spot where his fourth trap was set.

"Pike Liddicoat!" he muttered in astonishment and wiped a wet snowflake from his lips. "If he's stolen from my traps . . ."

He headed for the old tree on a dead run. The snow around the roots hadn't been disturbed, yet the trap was sprung and empty.

Probably sprung it with a stick, he thought angrily, opening it and baiting it again with the strip of fat pork. Just to be aggravating.

If he ever laid hands on the young skunk again, he'd teach him not to fool with the property of other folks. But what could you expect from somebody that ran around with the thieving Larkins?

He decided not to check the other traps, but follow young Liddicoat instead. If he had, some way or other, managed to get an animal out of that trap without leaving any signs of it . . .

Jon smelled the smoke before he saw the fire. Still it didn't prepare him for the sight that met his eyes when he reached the top of the knoll.

The Liddicoats might have been living in a fishnet for all the protection that the lean-to afforded them. A three-sided brush hut, it was made of poles lashed together with vines, and brush stuck in between! Before the open side a fire smoldered.

From outside the circle of warmth thrown by the fire, Jon could hear the dull thud of an ax. He made out the thin figure of the girl in the ragged homespun dress. She was hacking away at a log twice as big around as she was. How had she ever cut that tree down?

Jon hurried toward the brush hut. The girl apparently neither saw nor heard him, for she kept on hacking. Silently he went up behind her, thrust his hand over her shoulder and caught the handle of the ax just as she was about to lift it. The girl twisted her head, her eyes wide with fright.

"Now, who do you think you be?" she screamed. Then she recognized him, and fright turned to scorn. "Oh, it's you!"

Wrenching the ax out of his grasp, she again started to lift it. Again he took hold of it, and pulled it from her hands.

"I'll cut that wood," he said firmly. "It's no job for a girl."

Her answer was to lunge for the ax. "I don't need help from the likes of you! I've been cutting wood enough to keep us warm, and no reason I can see for not doing it now."

Jon surveyed the meager pile of wood beside the fire. "You won't keep very warm, rate you're going," he said kindly. "Looks to me you could use some help here, even from the likes of me."

He ran a tentative finger over the blade of the ax. "Dull as a dough hammer," he said, thinking that Pike was off traipsing around in the woods while his sister did all the hard work. Another Dave? he wondered.

Her shoulders sagged then, and she looked close to tears. "I know it," she said dully, "but I can't sharpen it."

"We got a stone," he told her as he lifted the ax and let it come down on the log. "I'll sharpen it for you."

She didn't move, just stood there watching, with her thin hands clasped in the folds of her skirt.

"We don't like being beholden to anybody," she said finally as a piece of the log fell away. Jon set it up, split it into four parts, and threw it on the pile by the fire.

"Everybody is beholden to somebody," he said as he cut another. "Don't see why you should want to be different."

The girl bit her lip. Then she stiffened at the sound of the querulous voice coming from inside the lean-to: "Cindy, where are ye?"

"Here, Pa," the girl answered, and turned and hurried into the shelter. She returned soon, her face paler than usual and her voice trembling. "He's got the shakes again," she said in a hoarse whisper. "I can't stand to watch."

Jon nodded, sympathetic. He'd seen his own father in the throes of the shaking ager enough to know how she felt.

"It'll be over," he said, trying to be comforting. "He'll sweat it out and feel better."

"Until the next spell," she said bitterly. "Seems like a body gets the ager he never gets rid of it." She turned on Jon and stormed, "I wish we'd never come out here! Ma sickened and died on the raft, and now Pa's so sick he can't get about at all." She began to sob. "I wish we were still in North Carolina. We didn't have much, but we were all together."

Jon averted his eyes; he never could abide to see a woman cry. "I'm sorry about yesterday," he mumbled. "I never meant to add to your troubles."

Cindy's small chin rose. She sniffed good and hard, as though determined to cry no more. "It wasn't your fault," she said. "Pike's got no business with those Larkins. They're so full of brag and meanness. I told him to leave them alone, but he wouldn't listen."

She sighed then, a sound that went through Jon like a slate pencil drawn across the slate at home.

He cut a good stack of wood. Then he picked up his rifle, patted it, and winked at the boy about Uriah's age who was peeking out the door of the lean-to at him.

"I'll bring you back a big fat turkey," he promised. He started to leave, then stopped and added, "And I'll take that ax home and sharpen it."

➤Chapter-5➤

"I bin expectin' ye." Old Josh's voice was gruff as he opened the door in response to Jon's pounding. But the old woodranger wasn't as gruff as he sounded, Jon had learned some time back.

"I came soon's I had some news to tell." Jon tried to be gruff, too. Dave had accused him more than once of imitating the ways of the old man, and Dave was part right about this, Jon had to admit.

Men like Josh never talked much, spending so much of their time alone they'd grown accustomed to silence. Jon liked that. There was much too much clapperjawing going on at home, he often thought. It'd be good to get away with someone who could spend a whole evening saying nothing.

He blinked to adjust his eyes from the dazzling whiteness of the snow to the smoky murkiness inside the one-room cabin. The smell inside was pungent.

"I'm part Injun, part b'ar, and part skunk," Old Josh liked to say. That he was part Indian was easy to see from his high cheek bones, piercing black eyes, and straight hair that hung to his shoulders. And you got used to the smell inside his cabin if you stayed in it long enough.

Actually his father had been a French trapper, one of the many who had taken Indian women as wives. Josh knew the woods and the ways of the Indians and the white men, and seemed to get along well with both. Each winter he hunted and trapped and made enough to live on.

Such men were never meant to be farmers, Jon thought, no more than he was. Though there was cleared land about the old man's squatter cabin, he had never turned a spadeful. Meat was the mainstay of his diet, and it was plentiful in the woods. Anything else he needed he traded his furs for. He had spent most of his life around the knobs of the river the Indians called O-hi-o, and still liked to live there.

"Good fur-bearing animals thinned out around here so's it hardly pays a man to hunt and trap these parts anymore," he had said often to Jon that summer and early fall. "But there's still lots of 'em up north. That's why I'm going there when it gets cold and freezes over."

Jon had been delighted when the old man had suggested he go along. He had thought of nothing else ever since. Now it was a reality; they were almost on their way.

"Winter's settin' in all right," the old man said, rubbing his gnarled hands gleefully. "Ma say she could spare ye?"

Jon nodded, so full of happiness he had little room for speech. "Yep," he replied. "Got the field cleared yesterday, ready for plowing come spring."

"Good, good." Old Josh sounded pleased. Though he wasn't much for talking, he did seem to enjoy company as much as most anybody. "Ground should be froze good and solid in a week or so."

He pointed to an extra trencher visible beneath a greasy

buckskin shirt that lay on the floor before the fire. "Have some stew." He picked up another trencher and filled it from the contents of a blackened kettle that sat in the coals of the fire. Fishing a piece of meat out of it with his fingers, he ate noisily.

The stew didn't look nearly as tasty as Ma's, Jon thought; but this wasn't the time to be picky. He'd likely be eating a lot such in the winter months ahead. He dipped out some of the greasy stuff, picked out a piece of meat with his fingers, and ate noisily too. He could hear Ma saying, as she did sometimes, "Just because we live out here in the wilderness is no sign we have to act like heathens."

She owned twelve pewter spoons, and she made her family use them instead of their fingers. No wonder some of the neighbors, those who didn't bother about such niceties, thought her a bit queer and notiony.

"What Ma don't know won't hurt her any," Jon thought now. The stew didn't taste as bad as it looked, and he was hungry from all that wood chopping. He sat and ate, content. He liked coming into the cabin and not having Ma say, "Clean off your feet!" or "Brush that snow off outside."

A little more snow and dirt on the floor of Old Josh's cabin couldn't hurt any, Jon thought. The whole place was a clutter of traps and skins and such. But it was a man's clutter, and he vowed he liked it.

He had liked the old woodranger ever since last spring, when Jon had first seen him about the abandoned squatter's cabin in the woods. Old Josh had taken a liking to him, too. They fished and hunted together, and talked man to man.

The old man had hunted and trapped for furs all his life and knew every angle. "Best fur animals around here are gone," he'd told Jon. "Too many folks movin' in and killin' 'em, or chasin' 'em off. But there's plenty left up north, and what a body can't hunt or trap for himself, he can trade the Injuns for."

Now Old Josh tipped his trencher and drank the liquid with a loud slurp. "We'll stick along Eel River most the winter," he said, wiping his mouth with the back of his hand. "Come spring, we'll have a pirogue piled high with prime pelts, and we'll go downriver to the Wabash and sell 'em at Vincennes. Always found the best prices there."

Jon listened avidly. He saw himself floating downstream with a pile of gold coins in the front of their boat. He'd bring the money back in time to keep some land-hungry settler with no right to it except ready cash—or, worse still, some land speculator—from pulling their claim out from under them.

The family would look up to him then, and Dave would have to. With the land secure, Dave could work it while Jon continued to hunt and fish and live the way Old Josh did. Oh, he might help his father build that sawmill if Pa still wanted it.

The old man's voice changed, rousing Jon from his daydreams. "It won't be easy," he warned. "Territory's still full of Injuns, and lots of 'em don't feel too kindly toward the white man. Won't do for a young feller like you, who don't know 'em like I do, to take chances. But if you listen to an old man that's done a lot of tradin' and livin' with 'em, you'll come out all right."

"Don't fret about me," Jon answered, stretching out his legs and giving a contented sigh. "I kin take care of myself."

"You can still learn from them that's lived longer," Josh shot back.

"Oh, I don't aim to do anything rash." Jon decided he'd

better humor the old man, though he did sound like Ma sometimes, throwing up storm signals when there was no need. Once up north, though, he'd do pretty much as he pleased.

"Salt's best for tradin' among the Algonquins," Old Josh told him. "They cain't get enough of it. But take along other things, too, like knives and scissors and a bolt or two of strouding."

That sounded like sense, Jon thought; he'd remember that.

The old man tossed his empty trencher onto a ragged bearskin in the corner. "No beads," he said. "I never was one for cheatin' 'em, and they remember that."

"You can carry more beads than you can salt," Jon reminded him.

Josh nodded. "But I still say it's cheatin' 'em to give 'em trinkets for furs they worked hard to get." He stared into the fire, then said, as an afterthought, "I never trade 'em firewater either, 'cause I know what that stuff does to an Injun."

Jon stared at the grizzled old man. There was more to him than Jon ever suspected. Why, this old woodranger that other settlers scorned as a good-for-nothing had more honesty in him than some shoutin' Baptists he knew.

Finishing his stew, Jon tossed his trencher onto the bearskin, then rose to leave. "I've got enough pelts now," he said, "to get my trade goods with. And I got a horse spoke for."

Old Josh followed him to the door. "I got a pack critter too," he said. "When we get ready to come back we kin trade 'em to the Injuns for more furs."

At the edge of the tiny clearing, Jon turned to wave goodby. Then he plunged into the forest. It was still snowing, and a wind had sprung up and was drifting the snow.

The footprints he'd made on the way over were almost filled with it now.

He heard the gobble of wild turkeys coming from a snow-covered thicket along the creek. Through the snow he could see them, fat from berries and seeds they had been consuming all fall, huddled together under the branches. Jon walked away with three of them slung over his shoulder.

He left two of the turkeys at the Liddicoat hut.

"Thank ye," Cindy said, averting her eyes. She didn't act grateful, Jon thought, turning her back to him as though resentful at having to accept his generosity.

But Mr. Liddicoat was thankful enough. When Jon looked inside the hut the thin, wan-looking man, bundled beneath what looked like rags and bark in the corner, said, "We're mighty grateful to you, young man."

And Ted, the younger brother, smacked his lips and grinned, "Turkey stew, mmmm."

Pike was nowhere to be seen. He must be a queer one, Jon thought, to let his folks go hungry.

Cindy seemed to read his thoughts. "Pike said he'd bring us a turkey," she said defensively.

"He's bin sayin' that for three days," Ted piped up, his eyes still on the birds by the fire.

Cindy shot a look at Ted that clearly told him to hold his tongue. Jon turned to leave. What had got into the girl any-how? Before, when he had split the wood, she had seemed almost friendly.

Let her sulk, he decided; he didn't want to get tangled up with a girl anyhow. Josh didn't have a woman around, and that was the kind of life he wanted.

Dave was splitting firewood when Jon arrived back home.

At the sight of Jon, Dave stopped and leaned on his ax handle.

"Well, I'll be," he said. "Ol' Daniel Boone himself, and with a turkey too. And turkeys so scarce around here, all a body has to do is reach in a bush and grab one. Now, how about grabbin' an ax and helping me with this wood? It's a sight harder than trompin' over to Old Josh's cabin."

Every word his brother said pricked like a nettle. It was all Jon could do to keep from smacking that sassy face. But Ma would just jump on him if he did. So he stalked past Dave and into the cabin.

"Shake that snow off outside." His mother straightened up from the kettle she was stirring.

Jon gritted his teeth. It sure would be good to go off with Josh and not have to listen to all the clapperjawing that came his way at home.

"What'll I do with this turkey?" he asked, bound to get some credit for his efforts. He set his rifle by the door.

"Just leave it there by the door," his mother said. "I'll take care of it later."

Jon put it down and went back out to help Dave.

"How about helping me roll this backlog in?" Dave said.

"Good idea," Jon replied. "Glad you got one big enough to last a couple of days. Looks like this snow is goin' to keep up for a while."

"That's what I been thinking." Dave was amiable now.

Together they rolled the backlog to the doorway, then through it and into the big fireplace. That done, Dave went back to chopping while Jon lingered to tell his mother about the Liddicoats.

"They're bad off," he said. "They sure need all the help they can get."

"I've got a bearskin I can send over for the man," Ma said.

48

"And I'll send some root potions for his ager. And——"

A piercing scream from outside sent a spasm of fear across her face. "Dave . . ." she said huskily. "Something's happened to Dave."

Jon and his mother reached the door at the same time. Through the swirling snow they ran to where Dave lay, holding one foot from which blood gushed in a rich, red stream.

"My ax slipped," he whispered, his voice hoarse with fear. "I'm bleeding to death."

"No you're not." Jon's confidence was soothing. "We'll have it stopped in no time." And slipping one arm beneath Dave's shoulder and the other under his knees, Jon lifted him tenderly and carried him inside.

Only a week ago, Jon recalled, Jed Jason had cut himself so and had almost died before the flow of blood was stopped with spiderwebs laid on thickly.

Jon gently set his brother on a pallet hastily placed before the fire. Ma, white-faced, bathed the wound in hot vinegar water and bound it with a poultice of crushed ginseng leaves, not putting much store in cobwebs. Then she and Jon lifted Dave to a chair and propped his left foot on a stool.

"It's not a mortal wound, thank the good Lord," she said. "But it will take a while to heal."

It would be some time before Dave did much walking on that foot, Jon thought. He'd not be going north with Old Josh, after all. He might have known something would happen to prevent it, and that Dave would be the cause of it! It took a real effort not to let his feelings show.

➤Chapter-6➤

Mouse in the buttermilk,
Skip-to-my-Lou,
Mouse in the buttermilk,
Skip-to-my-Lou,
Mouse in the buttermilk,
Skip-to-my-Lou,
Skip-to-my-Lou, my darling!

Ma shot a glance at Jon. Sing, it said, to keep up Dave's spirits.

Jon opened his mouth and sang along with Ma, Emma, Uriah, and Dave. Pa whistled.

What about my spirits? Jon thought.

The lilting notes of the song died away. Dave let his home-made fiddle lie on his lap as he stared listlessly into the fire. The only sounds around the hearth were the scrape of the sheller in Pa's hand as it raked down an ear of corn, and the soft rattle of the kernels as they hit the basket. Soon these sounds were joined by the whir of Ma's spinning wheel and the click of Emma's knitting needles.

Suddenly Uriah spoke up. "While I was down on Turkey

Creek this morning, I saw some men going through the woods, carrying a rod and chain. What was they doing, Pa?"

A pained look flicked across Thomas Roberts' face. "Surveying, likely," he replied.

"Government surveyors," Mrs. Roberts added softly. "And that means . . ." Her voice trailed off.

". . . that this land will be up for grabs soon's winter's over," Jon finished bitterly.

Emma's needles clicked in rhythm with her words as she added, "If the Scribners haven't already bought it."

The gloom about the fire deepened. It was common knowledge that Joel, Abner, and Nathaniel Scribner weren't wasting any time acquiring land in the area, and they had plenty of cash for entrance fees.

"Well, there's nothing I can do about it . . . now," Jon said heavily.

To Dave, the words were like a hot poker prodding him.

"Why don't you come out and say I cut my foot on purpose!" he flared. "Just to stop you from goin' north with Old Josh. Why don't you, huh?"

Ma laid a restraining hand on his arm. "Now, Dave," she soothed, "Jon didn't say that."

"Well, he might as well have; he makes his thoughts so plain the way he looks and acts." Sobs broke forth from him then—big, racking sobs.

"Dave, I didn't mean . . ." Jon belatedly tried to make amends. Pa rested the corn sheller Dave had whittled out of wood on one knee. "If I could have built that sawmill before I went off to fight the Injuns . . ." his words ended with a sigh.

Dave's sobs stopped. "Why can't me and Jon build it, Pa?" he cried. "With you telling us how, why can't we?"

Pa looked thoughtful. "A sawmill takes sawblades and

such that have to be shipped from Pittsburgh," he said. "That takes cash money, too."

Jon's alarm settled. He'd much rather earn money in the forests than around a mill on the creek.

"I hear the Scribners want a sawmill in New Albany," Ma said.

"They'll get it, too," said Pa. "I just wish it was ours."

Gloomy silence took over again. The Scribner brothers would get their mill, all right. New Albany had been a raw wilderness when the brothers had arrived there three years ago. They had platted it and sold it in sections, and now it was a bustling village. It seemed to Jon that every time he went there a new store had been added. Already it was an important stop for boats in the river trade.

The Scribners' dream for the region was as big and bold as Pa's had been when he had first come. The difference was that now they owned their land—the part they hadn't already sold—while the Roberts family were still squatters.

Squatters! Jon hated that word. Why, they were no better off than the Liddicoats! The land under the snug cabin they were in right now didn't belong to them.

Suddenly Dave sat up straight. He wiggled his good foot, plucked his fiddle, and sang saucily:

> *Oh, Charlie's neat*
> *And Charlie's sweet*
> *And Charlie is a dandy.*
> *Charlie is a nice young man . . .*

A loud and insistent knock at the door stopped the song as suddenly as it had begun. Ma got up from her wheel in alarm.

52

"Put away your fiddle, Dave," she said quickly. "It's likely one of the Simonses come a'borrowin'."

Dave clucked his disgust, but he shoved his fiddle out of sight under a rough bench. "I can't see the sense in being so afraid of them seeing me playing a fiddle."

"Because they think it's sinful, that's why," Ma said. "And I can't see the sense in riling them, if we don't have to."

"Dog take what they think," Dave muttered stubbornly. "Besides, the Good Book says that David played his harp and God didn't tell him it was sinful."

"The Simonses don't look at it that way. They read the Bible by the light of their own fires."

Dave could be downright argufying when he wanted to be, Jon thought, though mostly with him. Seldom did Dave take it out on his mother. For once Jon agreed with his brother, but he was glad to see Ma could be firm with him when she wanted to.

Still, Dave wasn't convinced. His mother was at the door as he muttered, " 'Bout time they read it by the light of other folks' fires then."

Jon was right behind Ma when she opened the door. You had to be careful who was let into a cabin, and the caller might not be a Simons, after all.

The light from inside the cabin glowed just enough to reveal the frock-coated man who stood holding the rein of a horse.

Ma gasped. "Why, Mr. Jennings! What happened?" She pointed to the blood running freely from an ugly gash in the side of the man's head. With a handkerchief he was trying to stem the flow on his smooth-shaven cheek.

"Three young hardbats stopped me on the road," Jennings cried angrily. "Threw rocks and tried to pull me off my horse.

53

But I threw my portmanteau at the one trying to grab my horse's bridle. I knocked him down and got away."

Jonathan Jennings brushed past Jon and his mother, staggered to the hearth, and dropped down on the bench.

Emma fetched a clean cloth and hot water to bathe his face.

"Take care of the horse, Jon," Ma said briskly, "whilst I fix Mr. Jennings something to eat."

After rubbing down Jennings' horse and feeding it and seeing it had water for the night, Jon headed back to the cabin. A familiar smell greeted him the second he opened the door. The smell was delicious, but he couldn't stand to drink the stuff itself.

As usual, Mr. Jennings had brought along his own supply of coffee. Ma was now brewing some of it for him.

"Would anybody care for a cup?" Jennings asked, after he'd finished a fine meal of stew and cornbread.

"Thank you, I will," Ma accepted eagerly.

She was the only one who did. "Slops," Pa had snorted at his first—and last—taste of the bitter brown liquid some months earlier. Jon, Dave, and Emma had silently agreed with him, and Uriah hadn't even wanted to try it.

"Tastes worse'n some of Ma's herb potions," Dave announced after Mr. Jennings had left that first time. "Can't see why anybody'd want to drink it, 'less he was tryin' to cure something."

"I found it a pleasant drink," Ma had said. "Gives me a warm sort of glowy feeling. And I like tea, too. Anytime one of the folks stopping offers me some, I won't be the one to say no."

Jon saw the blissful look on Ma's face now as she sipped from the nogginful she had poured for herself.

One of these days, he determined, I'm going to trade a

couple of pelts for a sack of that stuff and give it to Ma. Gives her so much pleasure, it's a shame she can't have all she wants to drink.

It was only the affluent travelers who brought their supply of coffee along. Although an occasional shipment came into New Albany by boat, coffee was too dear for most settlers.

Jonathan Jennings could afford it. He had served four terms in Congress, though lately he had let it be known he did not want to go back to Washington from the Indiana Territory.

Jennings' winning smile and manner made him a very popular figure with the settlers, though some of his more aristocratic constituents called him a beardless boy.

"Any man who can handle an ax or scythe, or pitch in at a logrolling like Jennings, is no beardless boy," Tom Roberts declared more than once. "He'll get my vote anytime."

"And he's against slavery," Ma always added to Pa's statement. "I don't hold with one man owning another."

"Indiana's got to come in free," all their neighbors agreed.

As he drank his coffee, the sandy-haired Jennings read from a copy of the *Western Eagle* he had brought with him:

"The next Territorial Legislature, due to meet in a few weeks, intends to draw up a petition for statehood for Indiana and send it to the Congress in Washington."

Pa's sunken eyes gleamed with interest. He always perked up at mention of politics. "And there's no doubt," he said, "that you aim to help Congress pass that Enabling Act so's we can elect delegates to a constitutional covention in Corydon this summer."

"That's correct," Jennings said, sipping his coffee contentedly. "Then I'll announce myself a candidate for one of the delegates." He added thoughtfully, "I have decided that the welfare of Indiana is closer to my heart than the affairs of the nation."

Pa leaned forward. "Are you going to run for governor if it becomes a state?"

Mr. Jennings smiled. "It's too early to think of that," he said, though the idea pleased him and clearly had already occurred to him. Gingerly he touched the bruise on his forehead. "But I do know that once we are a state we can pass and enforce laws to deal with such lawless hardbats as the ones who set upon me tonight."

Ma finished her coffee and looked pleased. "It will be good," she said, "to go to your door day or night and open it without worrying about who you'll find there."

Jennings nodded vigorously. "And to travel the roads without fear of being beaten and robbed—or worse."

"Get a look at the ones who stopped you this evening?" Pa asked.

"No." Jennings shook his head. "It was dark, and they jumped out of bushes along the road, yelling and hollering and throwing rocks at the horse. Of course he reared. Then one grabbed for the bridle, and that was when I threw my portmanteau at him. The others were thrown off guard for a second, and I put spurs to my mount and we outran them." He smiled as he recalled the scene. "I lost two fine shirts my wife had just made me, and my razor and strop; but I knocked down the one after the bridle, so they didn't get away unscathed."

"It was likely the Larkins," Dave said.

His words jolted Jon. If true, had Pike Liddicoat been with them? If he had, then Cindy—oh, drat Cindy! Why should he care what happened to the Liddicoats? He remembered then that he had not brought home the ax he had promised to whet for her. He could see her now, hacking away at a log with the dull blade. With half his mind elsewhere, he listened to Pa and Mr. Jennings talk on. They discussed the move of the capital of the Indiana Territory from Vincennes to Corydon.

"More central location," Jennings said.

Roberts nodded his agreement. "But we don't need that fancy building they put up in Corydon," he argued. "All stone, and costing six thousand dollars, I've heard."

"Ah, but prosperity will be the lot of everybody next spring," Jennings promised. "All the land hereabouts will be surveyed, and the land office will do a rushing business as folks start pouring in." If he noticed the gloom on the faces of his hosts, he did not show it.

"You can sleep right here on a pallet before the fire," Ma told him, "or you can sleep in the loft with the boys."

"I'll sleep with the boys."

Jon and Dave exchanged glances. Dave pulled a long face. Mr. Jennings snored loud enough to lift the rafters!

Only one snore Jon could remember was louder. That was the snore he had once heard when he had walked into a cave occupied, to his surprise, by a huge shaggy bear.

I wish I could get out of here as quick as I got out of that cave, he thought later as he lay with his hands clasped behind his head, staring up at the rafters of the loft. Where in the world was he going to get the money for that entrance fee? He had to get it; no one else in the family could.

He'd bet he was the only one worrying about it. Then he heard a hoarse whisper. "I'm sorry about cutting my foot, Jon."

A lump as big as a walnut formed in Jon's throat. He reached over and squeezed his brother's arm affectionately. "It'll all come out right, Dave. Don't fret."

He wished he felt as confident as he sounded.

➤Chapter-7➤

Jon was up early next morning. There was a lot to do, and now he was the only one who could do it. He looked down at the still-sleeping Dave. Let him rest, he thought; it will make his foot heal faster.

The form next to Dave was stirring. Mr. Jennings would soon be up, so he'd best make haste.

Down the loft ladder he went, feeling almost cheerful for some reason he could not figure out. The sight of the fire blazing on the hearth and Ma stirring the porridge in the iron kettle made him feel warm and good all over.

A home and a hearth of their own. How lucky the Roberts family was. Of their own? But this wasn't theirs and wouldn't be until . . . His spirits plummeted. And small chance he had now of doing anything about the situation.

But he wouldn't let Ma know how he felt, not this morning. Mr. Jennings would soon be down for breakfast.

Ma set a bowl of porridge on the trestle table. A pitcher of milk was already there.

"Mr. Jennings will be leaving soon as he eats," she said.

Jon nodded. "I'll have his horse fed and ready for him."

A short time later he and his mother stood in the doorway and watched as Mr. Jennings started down the narrow, rutted road toward Jeffersonville.

"I sure hope he's one of the delegates," Ma said as they turned back into the cabin.

"He will be if I have anything to say about it," Pa spoke up. He had come out early and was finishing his meal. Minutes before, he and Mr. Jennings had been talking politics as fast as both could go.

Pa would have had plenty to say, Jon knew. Made no difference to Pa which side of the political fence a guest was on, either; he stated his views bluntly.

"More'n one traveler has got so mad at your pa he's stomped out," Ma had told him once.

Ma had more than her share of troubles, he thought as he watched her drop the coins she had received from Mr. Jennings in a gourd she kept hidden behind a loose stone in the chimney. It would take forever for those coins to amount to enough. . . . Gruffly Jon said, "I better go tell Old Josh I won't be going with him."

Ma turned wearily. "Dave is mighty sorry for what happened."

"I know he is," Jon replied. "But that don't change things any—'bout my going, I mean."

Ma frowned and brushed back a lock of hair. "Now, I wouldn't say for sure certain your plans need changing," she said softly. "Dave's foot might be healed enough in a few days. You two weren't going to leave right away, were you?"

Jon's heart took a joyful leap. "You mean . . . not with my sorry luck . . ." He bit off the words before he said more than he meant to.

"Your luck is no sorrier than anybody else's," Ma told him.

"It's just your thinking makes it seem so. Anyway, take that bearskin in the corner to that poor Mr. Liddicoat. With ager he needs warm covers. And that noggin there is full of ginseng potion that's so good for the shakes. And there's a pone of cornbread . . ."

"Anything else?" Jon smiled in spite of himself.

"I just hope she leaves me something to eat," Dave said, hobbling down the ladder.

"Foot hurt?" Ma asked anxiously.

"Oh, a little." Dave shrugged. He didn't want to worry Ma.

"I'll put more poultice on it soon's you're through eating."

Dave wrinkled his nose. That poultice smelled pretty awful. "Sure the cure ain't worse'n the cut?"

"Dave, this is no funning matter."

"I know that." Dave looked at Jon as his brother slipped into his deerskin jacket and picked up all the truck Ma wanted him to take to the Liddicoats. "I want my foot healed more'n anybody. It's no fun hobbling around like a one-legged duck."

Jon shot him a grateful look. Maybe Dave's will to heal would help matters.

Taking his rifle, he went out the door almost staggering under his load. Wouldn't do to meet up with the Larkins now, he thought. He'd be helpless to stop them from taking this stuff.

Had Pike and the Larkins been the ones to set on Mr. Jennings? Likely he'd never know for sure.

He shifted the weight of the heavy bearskin. Then the noggin began to slip. And the cornbread . . .

"Drat it," he snorted as he stopped beside a fallen tree and set all the things on it. "Taking all this to that skunk's family while he's probably out robbing and worse."

Still, he wasn't certain sure it was the Larkins who'd tried

60

to rob Mr. Jennings. Or even if Pike had been with them. For Cindy's sake, he hoped Pike had had no part in it. Pike's folks weren't the Larkin kind.

Rearranging his stuff, he went on his way. He'd look at his traps on the way back. And this time he'd not forget that ax that needed sharpening. He hoped Cindy hadn't had to cut any wood with it since he'd seen her. Surely he'd left enough to last her until today.

Pike wasn't around the traps he passed this morning; that was some consolation. He wasn't around the lean-to either when Jon arrived. But the others were huddled around the fire trying to keep warm.

Cindy looked up dully. "Mornin'," she said without enthusiasm.

"Brought some things for you," Jon said pleasantly as he let Ted take the noggin and cornbread. Then he wrapped the bearskin around the thin shoulders of Cindy's pa. It was big enough to cover him front and back.

Mr. Liddicoat looked up gratefully. In a weak voice he said, "I sure do thank you."

Ted handed the noggin and bread to his sister and crawled under the bearskin with his father. He stuck his small shaggy head out through the front and grinned, showing where two teeth were missing.

"Warmest place I've found in a long time." He whooped and snuggled against his father.

Cindy's eyes were moist as she watched. "I thank you too," she said in a low tone, and held up the noggin. "This for Pa?"

Jon nodded. "Best thing there is for ager, Ma says."

"Then I'll take it," Mr. Liddicoat said. And as Cindy held the noggin to his mouth he drank a deep draught. Jon looked past them into the half hut. It was surprisingly neat and clean.

Then his eyes spotted something in one corner of it: a leather portmanteau with the initials J. J. carved plainly on one side!

Cindy saw what he was looking at. "Pike found it," she said. "He said it was setting right in the middle of the road. Figured some traveler must have dropped it, without knowing, and rode on. He brought it here 'cause he thought nobody'd want it, he said."

Jon swallowed hard. Pike had found it, had he? Didn't know who had dropped it, didn't he? The lying skunk! He'd been the one Mr. Jennings had knocked down with it, Jon would bet!

Words pressed hot against his lips. But somehow he kept them back. This whole family was no better than the Larkins, taking . . . thieving. . . . He felt like snatching up the bearskin and cornbread and taking them back home. They had to work for what they got, the Roberts family did. Why should they give anything to those who stole what they wanted?

Then he caught sight of little Ted snuggled blissfully beneath the bearskin. And he saw Cindy break off a piece of the cornbread and give it to her father. Two wrongs would not make a right, he thought, and it would surely be wrong to take away stuff so badly needed here.

"I'll pick up that ax on the way back," he said gruffly, pointing to it. "And I'll take it home and hone an edge on it."

"It needs it," Cindy admitted. And the hope that had crept into her face and voice during the last few moments convinced him he had been wrong about Cindy and her father and young Ted.

"Bring us another turkey?" Ted asked, grinning up at him from the folds of the bearskin. "That last one tasted mighty fine."

"I'll bring a fatter one this time," Jon promised, and strode

62

off. But he had the uncomfortable feeling he was being taken in, that they were laughing at him behind his back.

Pike was the one who had grabbed Mr. Jennings' bridle, he was almost certain of it. Cindy's older brother was as bad as the Larkins, and they were the worst on the frontier, worse even than the Indians, harming their own kind.

Still, Pike didn't look like a hardbat. Maybe he'd have a talk with Cindy's brother, point out that he'd come to no good if he kept on running around with the Larkins.

Best mind my own business, he thought as he reached the top of the knoll and started down toward Old Josh's cabin.

Josh listened gravely while Jon told him of Dave's injured foot and how it had likely changed his plans to go north.

The old woodranger scratched his head before he replied, "Your ma may be right. Dave's foot might heal faster'n you think. Anyhow, I won't be going for a few days, so we'll just wait and see."

Jon felt grateful. There was still a chance he might get to go, though a faint one. The old man was disappointed too, and that helped. Maybe he'd make allowances . . .

Jon felt some better on his way back. He shot two fat turkeys and stopped by the Liddicoats with them. There he picked up the dull ax. His eyes again fastened on the portmanteau with J. J. carved on one side.

"I think I know who lost that," he said. "Man stopped at our place last night and said he'd lost one just like it."

"Then take it to him." Cindy snatched it up and handed it to Jon. "We don't have any use for it. Pike didn't pick it up because he wanted it or the two nice shirts and razor and strop inside. He just figgered it was foolish to let it set there in the road." The look she gave him was straight and direct. It told Jon plainly that she believed every word of Pike's lie.

►Chapter-8►

It was several days later that Ma said happily, "Dave's foot is healing clean, with no sign of fester."

Jon eased the backlog into the fireplace. He pushed smaller pieces of wood close to it and flames licked up through them. It would soon catch fire and last for two days, at least.

He straightened up slowly, trying to keep his hopes from rising with the same high flare as the flames. "You mean he's not going to be laid up much longer?" he asked as casually as he could.

"He'll be walking around on that foot in a day or so, good as new," she said proudly.

Dave spoke up then, and he sounded happy too. "I'll be out in the woods shooting turkey and rabbit and squirrel and deer before you know it."

"No bear?" Jon teased, suddenly feeling lightheaded.

Dave looked him over coolly. "Not 'less'n I have to shoot one before he makes a meal of me," he said.

Dave had been mortally afraid of bears ever since one had surprised him while he'd been picking berries along the creek the summer before. "He was so close he slobbered on me!"

Dave had cried as he reached the cabin and slid into the cook-room on the seat of his deerskin pants. "I got away, though, before he could grab me."

"And left him a whole bucket of berries." Jon had laughed at his brother then, he had looked so comical on the floor. "And Emma counting on making a berry dodger for supper."

"She wants berries for a dodger, she can go get 'em," Dave had replied grimly.

It wasn't really a funny matter, Jon knew. Jon kept a wary eye out for the huge creatures. He had shot a few, and they had provided a lot of meat for the Robertses and their neigh-bors, as well as fine robes, one of which was around Mr. Liddicoat right now.

Dave pushed back his skin cap. He was feeling good this morning. "And I'll even watch your old traps and stretch and cure the hides I find in 'em," he said expansively.

Jon felt a sudden surge of warmth for his young brother. Then his better judgment came to the fore. Dave made such promises only to forget them later; he was as rattleheaded as a dried gourd.

"Might as well go get your trade goods, Jon," Mrs. Roberts broke in.

"I'll get my skins and get down to the store fast as shanks' mare will take me." Jon was gleeful.

"That ought to be right quick." Dave grinned, his eyes on Jon's long legs.

"And take that *Western Eagle*," Pa said, "and trade it for another paper."

"Be glad to." Jon laughed as he went up the loft ladder.

A few minutes later, newspaper folded beneath his shirt and a bundle of pelts thrown over his shoulder, Jon started happily for the barn.

Ma, at the last minute, had decided he should take a poke of corn to the mill to be ground. So he had to take Old Lightning to help him carry it.

Soon he and the old horse were slipping and sliding down the side of one of the knobs between the tavern and the village of New Albany. They teetered and swayed and braked themselves.

It had thawed some the day before and a light rain had fallen. The temperature had dropped below freezing in the early morning hours, and now there was a skimmer of ice underfoot.

Jon glowed so from the warmth of his sudden good fortune that he didn't feel the bite of the wind off the knobs. His feet felt as light as the occasional flake of snow now falling.

Cabins, nestling ever closer together, told him he was nearing the outskirts of the settlement. New Albany, he thought, was growing like a well-tended pumpkin vine. Its narrow lanes, like tendrils, reached out from the rutted main road, which paralleled the river. And along the road itself were small shops and places of business, new ones appearing every month, it seemed.

Jon passed a small cabin with a sign that read: JASON EDWARDS, HATMAKER.

"That wasn't there last time I came," he told Old Lightning. "Nor that." And he looked at another alongside whose bright new sign above the door proclaimed it to be the cooperage of JARED ADAMS AND SONS, BARRELS EXPERTLY FASHIONED, ETC.

"What we need now," he heard Clem Jepson say loudly, "is roads."

"Yer right," replied a bearded man, keeping an eye on the

scales on which Clem, the owner of the trading post, was weighing a big chunk of beeswax the man had brought in.

"Them Injun and buffalo trails jest ain't goin' to do when folks start settlin' further back from the river. It'll be too hard for them to bring their produce here to trade."

"Yer right." The bearded man nodded, satisfied with the price Clem offered him for the wax. Hefting an ax head lying on one end of the rough plank counter, he ran a thumb gingerly down its edge.

"Won't get them roads though," Clem said with a shake of his head, "till we're a state."

"Yer right." The man laid the ax before Clem, indicating he wanted it.

"And that can't come any too soon to suit me." Clem indicated the man still had a small item coming. "We've got sixty thousand people in the territory now, and that's what it takes for statehood. They do say——"

"Yer right." The bearded man picked up a big twist of chewing tobacco and his ax and went out the door.

"What kin I do for you, Jon?" Clem asked, turning to his only other customer. "*Eagle?*" he pointed to the corner of the newspaper protruding from the front of Jon's shirt. "Trade?"

Jon nodded.

"For this?" Clem pulled out a worn copy of the *Corydon Gazette* and held it up.

It was only a week old, and Jon knew neither Pa nor Ma had read it, nor had he.

"Done." Jon grinned and handed over the *Eagle*. He took the *Gazette* and, carefully folding it, put it where the *Eagle* had been.

"And here's a letter come fer yer ma a few days ago," Clem said, reaching up on a shelf behind him and taking down a small, sealed packet. He squinted at it. "From Kaintuck."

Jon knew it was from Aunt Jenny, Ma's sister. He wondered if she and her husband, Jeff, had decided to cross the river and settle in the Indiana Territory. He hoped so, for Ma's sake; she pined a lot for her young sister and the children. He put the letter inside his shirt front, with the newspaper.

"There'll be a lot of good reading around the fire tonight," he said, and threw his bundle of pelts on the counter.

Clem opened the bundle of furs—muskrat, raccoon, and a few beaver. He graded them according to size and primeness, running experienced fingers through their velvety softness. He gave his estimate of their worth.

"Best price ye'll git any place, young feller," he said, showing yellow stumps of teeth in a wide grin.

"Better than John Martin at Corydon?" Jon asked slyly.

Clem sent a stream of tobacco juice onto the dirt floor. "Lots better." He leaned across the counter. "What ye got in mind for trade?"

Jon doubted the price was better than Martin's. If he hadn't been in such a hurry to get going up north, he would have made the longer trip to Corydon and John Martin's trading post. John, he was sure, wasn't quite the skinflint Clem was.

Now he looked Clem in the eye as he said, "I want trade goods to take north with me."

"Oh, goin' up north, be ye?" Clem said. "Then ye'll want a lot o' these beads."

"No beads," Jon said firmly. The beads were bright and

cheap, and he was tempted. But he recalled what Old Josh had said. So he picked out awls, knives, and scissors.

"And I want some needles and a bolt of strouding," he said, pointing to the red and blue woolen cloth shipped clear from the English town of Stroud. Old Josh had said the Indians coveted this material. "And a bushel of salt."

"Jest got a boatload from Kaintuck," Clem said, and waved his hand toward a number of bushel sacks full of the precious stuff from the salt licks. When Jon had added one of them to his other purchases he fairly staggered under the weight.

Going through the doorway he collided with somebody.

"Watch where you're going," he said with good humor. "I can't."

Looking over the bolt of strouding he found himself gazing into a familiar face, now with an ugly gash below the heavily fringed left eye.

"Think you own the earth?" Pike asked sullenly.

Over Pike's shoulder was a small bundle of pelts, mostly raccoon. Jon's brief glance at them was enough to spark Pike's resentment.

"They didn't come from your traps, if that's what you're thinking," he snarled.

"I'm just thinking I'd like to get out of here," Jon replied, staring hard at Pike standing, feet wide apart, in the middle of the doorway.

But Pike seemed determined to have his say. "Ever since you saw me by your trap along the creek you've been thinking I took something out of it—right?"

Jon just leveled his glance at the bruise on Pike's cheek.

"Run into a tree or something?" he asked mildly. Nothing could rile him this morning.

Pike went right on. "I had a trap of my own set up the creek a ways from yours. I saw something had been taken from it. So I went down to your trap to see if the same thing had happened there. I saw you then and knew what you'd think. So I just ran."

Pike shifted his weight uneasily. "I got a good idea who done the stealing," he said, "but there ain't one thing I can do about it."

Then he turned almost civil. "I only got two traps, and that's where I got these critters. I aim to get some powder and shot in trade and go out and git some meat. Much obliged for the turkeys."

He brushed past Jon then and disappeared into the shadows of the store.

"You're right welcome," Jon called after him. "Tell Cindy I'll bring her ax soon."

He took long strides up the road toward the gristmill, where he had left the corn and Old Lightning. Pike's story of the furs sounded so truthful. But was it? He had told Cindy he found the portmanteau in the road. And Jon was now doubly certain that he hadn't. He had got that gash under his eye when Mr. Jennings knocked him to the ground with the satchel.

"I've still got no use for him," Jon thought as he neared the mill.

"Ye'll have to wait a short spell," the miller told him. "Got one other customer ahead of ye."

"That's fine with me," Jon said. He eased his trade goods down beside the customer's bench and sat down. "I'm in no rush."

It was pleasant to sit there, let his thoughts wander, and

savor the pleasure of things turning out right for him for a change.

The wait was indeed a short one. In no time the miller had taken out his toll and poured the rest of the meal into the corn sack.

Jon was lifting the sack onto Old Lightning when he saw Pike walk by.

Young Liddicoat's head was bent to the stinging wind. Long strands of lank hair flew out from beneath his frayed cap. His thin shoulders were hunched into a ragged shirt; over this he wore an ancient deerskin jacket, obviously discarded by someone much larger than he.

Even while he was tying the sack on one side of the horse to balance the bolt of strouding and the rest of the trade goods on the other, Jon's eyes were on Liddicoat. Pike looked just like Cindy, he thought, thin and puny. His feelings toward her brother softened. He spoke up loud and clear: "Get your powder and shot?"

Pike's head jerked up like a startled fawn's.

"That's what I came for; that's what I got." But he slowed down and waited.

Jon took the old horse's reins and caught up with Pike.

"Aimin' to hunt this winter, are you?" he asked, for something to say.

Pike flared at that. "I'm aimin' to keep us in meat from now on, if that's what you mean."

"Oh, I wasn't meaning anything in particular," Jon replied. Pike and Cindy were much alike, touchy and quick to anger. "I'm going up north for furs," he said. "Be gone most of the winter."

Pike turned then, his eyes bright with curiosity and envy.

"Is that a fact? By yourself?"

"Nope. With Old Josh."

"The old coot that lives up by the creek by himself?"

Jon nodded. Old Josh wouldn't mind being called that. Often called himself an old skunk.

"Wish I could go with you. Maybe then I could . . ."

"I'm going for pelts to sell for enough cash money to pay the entrance fee on our land," Jon said, feeling almost friendly toward Cindy's brother now. He couldn't really be evil, this soft-voiced, white-faced lad. Jon expanded. "And I'm going to buy the iron parts for a sawmill Pa aims to build."

This last was a new thought. Pa would have been surprised had he heard it.

"A sawmill!" Pike cried. Then he turned wistful. "My pa worked at a sawmill back east. Those were good times. We had a nice cabin like yours, and Ma was alive then, and we had plenty to eat."

Pike's sigh was close to being a sob. Then came a loud snuff and a stiffening, as though to hold back a torrent of tears.

"I reckon we'll always be squatters," he said bitterly, "way things are going now." He shifted his old rifle and strode on, sullen once more.

Snow drifted down as they walked on silently for a while. It fluttered down so fast the flakes partly obscured their vision. Jon, busy with his thoughts, wasn't paying any attention to where he was going. If the Liddicoats were driven off the land where they were living this winter, he thought, Cindy would go with them. He wouldn't like that.

Before he realized it, he and Pike had veered off the route to the tavern. Stopping briefly on the top of a knob, he saw he was a half mile off his course, and Pike was that much closer to the Liddicoat lean-to.

"Take care," Pike said as they parted and headed in different directions. "If I don't see you again before you leave, best of luck."

"Thank you kindly," Jon replied, his hand firmly on Old Lightning's rein, the frosting of snow on the icy glaze making footing more treacherous than ever. "I hope you have turkey and deer in the pot every day."

Both laughed and waved at each other.

Jon had just forded the creek when a burly figure rose up from behind a fallen log. At the same time another appeared through the snow on the other side. Dimly he saw Pike's figure in the distance.

Pike and the Larkins! What a fool he had been to walk right into their trap. A heavy object landed on his skull then, and a thousand lights flashed and were snuffed out. He could feel himself floating . . . falling, just before he lost all power to think or feel.

➤Chapter-9➤

As though through a fog, the familiar harsh voices came through to Jon.

"Must be a bushel o' salt here! An' meal fer a month."

"An' trade goods that'll bring a pretty penny in Corydon."

The Larkins! Glazed though his vision was, Jon could make out Pike's face, white and scared near by.

"Git goin', Liddicoat," one of the Larkins snarled. "When we need ye, we'll let ye know."

A rustle told Jon that Pike had taken off like a scared rabbit. Then he heard the faint whinny of a horse. Old Lightning.

"Let the nag go. We don't need him."

He'd go home, Jon thought. Old Lightning would go straight home. Drowsiness took a firm grip, pulled him down, down, down. How nice to go to sleep. . . .

"Glory be, he's coming round," his mother's voice was saying.

Jon opened his eyes. He blinked, and his surroundings came into focus. Ma was bending over him. Dave, Emma, Uriah, and Pa were hovering about.

"How'd I get here?" he asked, bewildered.

"It was the Lord's will sent your horse home," a familiar voice came from beside the fireplace. And John Simons' eyes looked piously upward.

"Soon's he got here we started out looking for you, Ma and me." Dave grinned down at him. "You were an armful to bring back, all right."

"What *did* happen?" Ma asked anxiously.

Jon closed his eyes for a second. The whole chain of events passed before him. Pike was to blame. He and the Larkins had met in New Albany, had planned the whole thing. Pike had told them about his trade goods and meal, then had led him into their trap.

"The Larkins did it," he muttered. "The skunks."

A stab of pain shot through him that was not caused by the swollen knot on his head. Trade goods gone, he could not go north with Old Josh.

Ma knew what he was thinking and asked no more questions. Gently she pressed a warm poultice against his throbbing head. But the others talked angrily.

"Until we get some laws here, and jails to put the likes of the Larkins in, such as this will keep right on," Pa said, his voice vibrating with indignation.

Grim-faced, Simons got up from the three-legged stool. "We'll just have to take things into our own hands until then," he said. "The Bible says an eye for an eye. . . ."

"What do you propose?"

"Drive the Larkins out, same's we did the Indians. . . ."

And the Liddicoats, too, Jon thought. Pike had as much to do with this as the Larkins had. But then Cindy . . . He'd not say anything about Pike just yet.

A pounding came from outside the cabin door.

Dave limped to the door, swung it open, and stared at the thin, white-faced young man who stood outside.

"Kin I come in?" Pike's voice was shrill with fear.

Jon rolled over, faced the door. Well, Pike Liddicoat had nerve, all right, coming here after what had just happened along the creek.

"Of course," Dave replied, and stepped aside for Pike to enter.

Pike looked around nervously before he walked in. What did he expect to see?

The atmosphere inside the cabin was tense and hostile. Everyone knew who Pike was, that he had been one of the three who had disrupted the logrolling. Any sympathy they might have for the rest of his family was not wasted on Pike.

"What do you want?" Pa's voice was brittle with suspicion.

Pike blinked snowflakes from his long lashes. He shifted from one bark-covered foot to the other.

"Wanted to see if he got home all right, for one thing," he jerked his head in Jon's direction.

"That's right nice of you." Ma's voice was civil enough.

Jon almost blurted out his own feelings, but somehow Pike made him think of Cindy standing there, proud and pitiful. He set his lips together tight, let none of the hot retort come through them.

To his surprise, Pike came over to him, looked down, and winced at sight of his bruised and blackened face. Then Pike blurted out, "Soon's I knowed they were good and gone, I came back to see if I could he'p you," and he sounded earnest enough. "When I got there, your ma and brother were carrying you away."

"Is that a fact?" Jon was sarcastic in spite of himself. This close, Pike looked nothing like Cindy.

76

Pike drew in his breath, looking resigned to Jon's reception of his story. Then he shrugged and went on doggedly. "When I saw you were all right I took out after them. I had a hunch where they'd put that truck of yours."

Jon perked up. Was there a chance of getting his trade goods back? Pike was probably just leading him on, maybe into another trap.

But Pike had started and couldn't stop.

"It's a dugout they got along the creek. They was just leaving it when I got within seeing distance. I waited until they were good and gone, and then I looked inside. There was the salt and meal and trade goods they took from you, stored inside."

Jon sat up. He wanted to believe Pike; he wanted to believe him the worst way. He wanted those trade goods back, and in getting them he wouldn't count the cost too dear.

Pike twisted his hands together.

"Don't tell a soul I told you this," he quavered, looking pleadingly around at the others, then back to Jon. "If you swear you won't, I'll tell you where the dugout is. And if you hustle, maybe you can get your trade goods back."

"I'll not tell," Jon said eagerly. "The others won't either."

Pike, reassured, went on.

"Recollect where the trap was you saw me by that morning?"

"I recollect."

"From there, bear to yer right up the creek for a quarter mile and you'll find another tree with roots growing outside just like that'n does. Crawl back under into the bank and you'll find a dugout there as dry as a bone. You'll find your stuff there, too. But only as long as it takes them to decide to move it. And that can be right quick."

Jon nodded. "I'll go after it right away."

Pike nodded, seemingly relieved to have it off his chest. Then he turned, sending pleading looks around the room.

"I'm leavin' now," he said softly. "I just hope they didn't see me come in. And I hope you all recollect you promised me not to say a word about my being here."

Everybody nodded solemnly. "We're folks that keep our word," Ma said, "and we all have long memories."

Jon wondered how Ma meant that, but he didn't say anything. They watched silently as Pike slipped out the door and into the falling snow.

As soon as the door had shut behind Pike, Pa spoke up: "Who is *they*?"

"The Larkins, of course," Jon replied, but added nothing more. To do so would disclose Pike's part in the whole sorry thing, and he wasn't quite ready to do that.

"I don't trust him," Dave said firmly. "Bet he knows more'n he's letting on."

"He's a fair-looking boy," Emma said softly.

They looked at her in surprise. It was the first time she had ever noticed a boy before, at least to say anything about him.

Jon shook his head to rid himself of dizziness.

"I'm starting out first thing in the morning," he said, "to look for my trade goods."

By morning a fluffy layer of snow lay on top of the frozen crust already covering the ground.

"Now don't fret, Ma," Jon said as he rose from the trestle table and his morning meal. "Lightning don't strike twice in the same place."

"I've known it to," Ma replied. She turned, and Jon could

78

see the worry lines creasing her forehead. "I'd almost rather they kept that salt and truck."

"I wouldn't." Jon was grim. "I need them to go north for furs. And I need the furs for——"

"I know, I know."

Jon turned to Emma. "Don't go setting your cap for that Pike," he said.

Emma looked at him archly. "And you stop going by to see his sister," she snapped.

Jon slammed the door behind him. A body's family could sure be a trial sometimes. He headed for the shed where Old Lightning was kept. He'd need him to carry the salt and meal, same as he had yesterday.

In spite of his efforts to keep them at bay, fear and doubt gnawed at him with every step. He had no desire to meet up with the Larkin boys again. And he couldn't be sure Pike's story wasn't leading him into another trap. But why? The Larkins stood to gain nothing by attacking him this morning. Yet he knew their kind often struck just for the perverse pleasure it gave them to inflict pain on another human being.

None of it made sense to Jon. Still, he knew it was true, and it didn't make him feel any better about his excursion. But he couldn't pass up a chance to get back those trade goods. Too much depended on them.

He turned complete circles frequently, hoping to catch anything that might be approaching from the rear. He stayed away from clumps of snow-laden bushes, fallen logs, and stumps.

Reaching the creek, he crossed it by jumping from rock to rock in the stream, narrowed now by ice along its edges. He passed the tree under which his trap still lay. He walked as warily as he would in summer, when the place was thick with massasaugas, or black rattlesnakes. The snakes might be hibernating, but the Larkins weren't. Old Lightning trudged patiently beside him.

He reached the tree Pike had told him about. A huge sycamore, its trunk was mottled by peeling bark. It was much bigger than the tree where his trap was hidden, and the roots were longer and reached farther. Underneath was a round-ceilinged cave of sorts.

Looking around, he noted no fresh footprints in the snow.

"Looks like we're the first ones here this morning," he told Old Lightning. Stooping, he made his way underneath the tangle of roots and earth.

Some of the roots, he noticed, had been cut off with an ax. His heart thumped when he saw the sack of salt leaning against the far side. Piled beside it were the meal and the trade goods.

He knew why the Larkins had left it all here instead of taking it to their tumbledown shack a few miles away. They likely had stolen stuff hidden away in a dozen or more such spots. They often left their shack for days at a time. Probably by hiding their ill-gotten gains in several places, they could be assured of finding some of it when they returned.

Leaning his rifle against the wall, he grasped the bag of salt. He began to drag it back the way he had come. But just as he straightened up, outside the roots, he felt a heavy hand on his arm. Spinning around, he found himself looking into the small, piglike eyes of Chet Larkin.

"Git goin'," Chet snarled, "and we won't smash yer face agin." He tore the sack of salt from Jon's grasp.

Weak with fear for one fleeting second, Jon stiffened with anger and resentment.

"I'm only taking what you took from me," he replied grimly. "And what's more, I aim to keep it."

Chet clenched his huge fist and waved it before Jon's eyes. "Ye don't say," he sneered. "And jest how do ye aim to do that?"

Jon grabbed for the sack of salt. Foolish or not, it was something he had to do. Chet and Jed, who stood grinning foolishly beside his brother, closed in on him.

"Want a fight," Jed smirked, "we'll be happy to oblige."

"We'd like a good fight too," a deep voice boomed from somewhere behind the sycamore. Jon looked up. Looming there, as big as giants, stood Luke and Sam Simons!

"Yippee!" he yelled, loud enough to be heard in New Albany.

Chet and Jed whirled. They paled visibly as they saw they had more than met their match.

"Aw, we wuz jest funnin'," Jed whined.

"Git goin'," Sam snarled, and he and Luke jumped down beside Jon.

The Larkins turned and fled.

"They sure are bold and brave when they meet up with somebody their size, ain't they?" Luke grinned.

➤Chapter-10➤

"Pa told us last night what you aimed to do this morning," Sam said, as he picked up the bag of salt and threw it on the back of Old Lightning. "Where's the rest of the truck?"

"In there," Jon said.

"He said it was risky, your coming for your stuff by yourself," Sam went on as Luke went under the tree roots to get the meal and trade goods. "So he sent us over to help you out. But time we got to your cabin your ma said you'd left. So we follered your tracks. Got here just in time too, didn't we?"

"You sure did," Jon said thankfully.

Never again would he think an unkind thought about Mr. Simons. If the man wanted to frown on fiddle playing and such, that was his affair.

Luke brought out the rest of the stuff and tied it to the back of Old Lightning. Then all three started toward the Roberts home.

Never much at talking, Luke and Sam were silent most of the way. With each step, though, Jon's thoughts were darting about.

Somehow it looked as though the Larkins had known he

was coming for his stuff this morning. Almost seemed as if they'd been waiting for him. How they had come by that information was easy to figure out.

Pike! It had been one of the Larkins' cruel jokes to send Pike to his home last night to tell him where he could find his stolen goods. They were capable of such a trick, he knew; but Pike? He didn't seem to be that sort somehow. Or was he getting Pike and Cindy mixed up a bit? The whole thing had Jon's head awhirl.

Luke and Sam bade him goodby on the edge of the clearing behind his home. Jon knew why. Big bashful men, they would be embarrassed at the thanks Ma and the others would heap on them.

Jon gave them a wave and went on, winding through the tree stumps in the clearing. Dave would have a time plowing around them come spring. He was thankful it would be Dave doing it. About that time he'd be coming in with his big load of furs, which he'd sell for cash; then he would pay the entrance fee, and the family would be grateful to him.

Whistling, he stashed his salt and meal and trade goods inside. Then he announced he was going over to see Old Josh. He went out the door before Ma could stop him.

"Git in a fight with a b'ar?" Old Josh asked as Jon stepped inside the woodranger's cabin. He had walked as fast as he could to get there, his rifle at the ready. He'd known the risk he was taking. The Larkins, now as mad as swarming hornets, would get even with him, given a chance.

Jon, fingering the bruise on the side of his head, replied as lightly as he could. "Two of them," he said. "The Larkin boys."

Old Josh snorted. "Hit's a pity them two don't run into a couple o' hungry ones. Save the rest o' us a sight of trouble."

Then he looked questioningly at Jon to hear the reason for his coming. Jon leaned his rifle beside the fireplace. "Dave's foot's healing," he said quietly. "And I've got my trade goods. We can start north any time you say."

Under the bushy brows the old woodranger's faded eyes gleamed with pleasure. Rubbing his gnarled hands, he said, "No use wastin' time. Best be going the next day or so."

No sooner had he spoken than there was a shrill cry from outside, followed by a frantic pounding on the door. Old Josh opened the door a crack, then wide, and Pike Liddicoat almost fell into the room.

"They're after me," he gasped. "Don't let 'em git me!"

"Who's after ye?" Josh demanded.

"Jed and Chet Larkin." The white face turned to Jon. "They figured out how you knew where your truck was. Right away they come to the hut looking for me. I was out settin' traps, so they told Cindy they were out to kill me!"

"The dirty skunks," Old Josh spat out. "Worse'n the Injuns ever was."

Pike gulped. "They saw me a minute ago down by the creek and they started after me. This was the closest place I could think of to run to." The thin shoulders shook violently.

From outside came a bellow like that of a wounded bear: "Send Liddicoat out or we'll burn yer cabin down, ol' man!"

Josh looked grim. Through a slot in the door of the cabin Josh slid his rifle barrel. Putting his mouth close to the slot, he yelled, "Come one step closer and I'll shoot."

The threat stopped the Larkins, but they yelled back, "We'll git him! When he comes out we'll git him. We'll make him wish he'd never been borned!"

"I wish that now," Pike said bitterly. "What am I goin' to do? I cain't stay here forever."

Chapter Ten

Fear and doubt wiped out Jon's jubilation of a few minutes ago. He was to blame for Pike's predicament, he supposed. And what about Old Josh for the next couple of days?

"Don't fret about me none." The old man had read Jon's thoughts. "I've faced up to worse than this." He jerked his head Pike's way. "He kin stay here long's he wants to. Plenty to eat and wood for the fire."

Pike sighed. "I wish't I could," he said. "But I cain't leave Cindy to care for Pa and Ted all by herself."

You've done a good job of that so far, Jon started to say, but checked himself. He did have Pike to thank for getting his trade goods back. "I'll tell Cindy where you are," he offered. "Maybe in a day or so the Larkins'll forget."

Pike shook his head. "They never forget anything." He turned to Josh. "I'll stay here till dark, then make a run for it."

Rifle gripped firmly, Jon stepped outside. The Larkins had a score to settle with him too, and he must not forget it. Uneasily, he walked to the Liddicoat hut.

As he stepped into the circle of warmth surrounding the fire Cindy looked up startled. "Lord, I thought you were the Larkins!" she cried in relief.

Jon winced. The feelings of guilt he had been having since he left Old Josh's cabin sharpened. Was he doing the right thing, going north for furs? With him gone all winter Cindy would have no one to turn to. And what about Ma and Dave and the others at home? Could they cope with the meanness of the Larkins? Even he had needed Luke and Sam that morning. "What's there to be scared about?" he asked softly, squatting down beside her and Ted.

Her thin shoulders shuddered. "It's Pike," she whispered. "They're after him. And they'll get him, too." A dry sob shook her.

"Pike's all right now." He tried to calm her. "He's over at Old Josh's."

"They drove him there, didn't they?" Sheer terror was in her eyes.

Jon gulped. "He said to tell you he'd stay there . . ."

"Till he thinks he can get here all of a piece," Cindy said bitterly. She shrugged. "They'll get him; just give 'em time."

Without another glance at Jon, she began ladling some stew from the fire-blackened kettle into a wooden bowl. Then she rose and took it into the half hut.

"Here, Pa," he heard her say. "This'll warm you."

"Much obliged, Cindy."

Beside him, Jon saw Ted hunkering down a bit farther. His heart went out to the three of them. It was bad enough to have to depend on such a sorry shelter for protection against the biting cold. To live in terror of such as the Larkins was infinitely worse.

Wasn't there something he could do besides put meat in the cooking pot and wood on their fire? Suddenly an idea came to him. Why hadn't he thought of it before?

Old Josh's cabin would be empty all winter. The Liddicoats could live in it. Josh wouldn't mind, he was sure of that. The chinked-log walls would keep out the wind, and there was a hearth for a fire inside.

He rose, feeling better. When spring came and he got back he could call a cabin raising, and then the Liddicoats would have a cabin of their own.

But they had no land! That part of his plan collapsed like one of Uriah's corncob forts. Well, he'd cross that bridge when he came to it. At least they'd have a shelter during the winter. He'd not say anything to Cindy though, until he'd talked to Old Josh.

Ted looked up at him, eyes big and round and solemn.

"When I'm a man," he said grimly, "I'll run them Larkins into the river."

"And that's where they should be," Jon replied, "a lot sooner than that."

He left then. There wasn't anything else he could do. But before he left with Old Josh he'd see to it that Cindy and her family were snug in the old woodranger's cabin.

Every step he took was cautious. Rifle ready to raise at the slightest warning, he swung his gaze warily from side to side and back over his shoulder. He kept a safe distance from snow-covered clumps and logs and stumps. No telling when Jed or Chet would rise from behind one of them.

It was an awful thing, this living in constant fear of attack from one's own kind. How much longer could it go on? He'd be safe enough from the Larkins after he had left with Old Josh. But what about the others?

Worry gnawed at him. The sight of the big log cabin warmed him inside. Guard relaxed, he hastened toward it.

His spirits fell the instant he opened the door. Pa, Uriah, and Emma were hunched before the fire, as worried-looking as Cindy had been.

"Where's Ma and Dave?" he asked in alarm.

Pa pointed to a pallet beside the hearth. Jon's hasty glance took in his brother lying there, face as bruised and swollen as his own had been.

"He was down by the creek settin' a trap," Pa said. "Chet and Jed set on him something terrible."

"It put Ma in a state," Emma added. "She said something had to be done about the Larkins, if she had to do it herself. She lit out for the Barkuses to see if they and some of the others'd help her."

87

Ma was right, Jon thought. A body could take just so much. "I'm going after her," he muttered and went out.

Cold anger stalked with him. It was time he and the others stopped being afraid of a couple of hardbats and put the fear of the Lord into them.

Last summer, he thought grimly as he strode toward the Barkus cabin, the Larkins had started their reign of terror. A preacher had come into the settlement for a camp meeting. Folks had flocked in to hear him. They had come on foot, on horseback, and by wagon. The horses had been tied in a grove by the creek that ran through New Albany.

Suddenly, during one of the gatherings, whooping and screeching and cursing had been heard outside. Some of those in the leaf, twig, and sapling tent had rushed outside just in time to see Chet and Jed driving off several of the horses.

It had broken up the camp meeting for good; horses were too precious to lose. Since then, the Larkins had struck again and again. They stole or chased off a pig here, a horse or cow there. They set fire to sheds and let animals out of pens. They attacked travelers and those they met in the woods alone. And no one, so far, had done anything about them except talk.

Jon kept an anxious eye on his mother's footprints in the snow. So long as there were no other prints he had no cause to fear for her.

All along the Ohio River there lived characters as bad as, or worse than, the Larkins. They sank boats and rafts, killing the passengers and stealing their goods. Hiding out in caves in the bluffs along the bank of the river, they boasted that no one could touch them. They'd keep on, just like the Larkins, as long as they could get away with it.

Jon's pace quickened. He couldn't leave with Old Josh until something had been done about the Larkins. He thought of the day of the logrolling when Pike had been with them. He saw again the satchel in the lean-to. How much was Pike involved with them? Was his running into Old Josh's cabin today another one of his tricks? He shook his head to rid it of such a thought. Pike's terror had seemed real enough.

The Barkus cabin came into view, and Jon sighed with relief. Ma's footprints led right to the door.

He knocked loud enough so he could be heard above the angry babble of voices coming from inside. Ma's voice sounded above all the rest.

"There's more of us than there is of them," he heard her say. "They ought to get a dose of their own potion." She whirled as Jon came through the door. "Oh, thank the Lord, they didn't get you, Jon!"

She embraced him and kissed his cheek right in front of all the Barkuses. Jon could have gone right through the puncheon floor with embarrassment.

Mrs. Barkus smiled at him; her husband and Mark nodded greetings.

Les Barkus spoke up. "Yer ma's been saying we ought to do something about them Larkins, Jon, and I think she's right. So long as we set like a bunch of scared rabbits and do nothing, they'll keep right on with their devilment."

Jon nodded. "What'll we do?" he asked.

"We'll round up the Simonses and some of the other neighbors," Barkus replied, taking down his rifle and powder horn, "and we'll smoke them snakes outen their hole."

John Simons and Sam and Luke gladly joined them; so did Ed Lyons and Doug. Grimly they bore down on the Larkin shack, situated several miles up the creek. Jed and Chet lived there with their father, as shiftless and worthless a character as had yet come into the territory.

As stealthily as Indians they sneaked up and surrounded the shack before the three inside knew what was happening.

Together Mr. Barkus, Luke and Sam put their shoulders to the half-rotten door and forced it open. The three Larkins jumped up from the rough bench set before the fire, where they'd been eating stew from a common pot on the hearth.

Jon noted with satisfaction how the eyes of Chet and Jed bugged with terror.

"Whatcha gonna do?" whined Chet, seeing the odds were overwhelmingly against any resistance on their part.

"What we shoulda done a while back," Barkus answered. "Give ye a dose o' yer own potion, only bigger."

On the way, Jon had listened to Barkus and Simons agree upon the punishment they would mete out. It turned his stomach at first. Old Man Larkin, the men said, had taught Chet and Jed all they knew about meanness. He was as guilty as they.

"Them as show no mercy should git no mercy," Barkus reminded him.

"An eye for an eye, the Good Book says," Simons had added.

It was frontier justice, Jon knew, and had been practiced before.

They dragged the Larkins out of their shack and tied them to three large trees near a small clearing, tied them securely with rawhide thongs that bit into the flesh when they moved even slightly. Then they set fire to their shack and left them howling there.

"They'll either starve or freeze or get et by bears," Barkus said as they left. "Nobody's likely to come by and feel sorry for 'em and cut 'em loose."

➤Chapter- 11➤

"Take care, Jon," Ma said softly and kissed his cheek. Then she turned hastily and went back into the cabin.

A burning sensation, compounded of anxiety and regret, rose from the pit of Jon's stomach and ended in his throat.

"I will, Ma," he said, averting his tear-stung eyes from the others. He should be happy as all get-out this morning.

Pa slapped him on the back and followed Ma's advice with "Keep an eye out for the Injuns, son. A lot of them still recollect how we took their hunting grounds away from 'em and are spoiling for a chance to get even."

"I will, Pa," Jon promised again. He turned to Dave. "Take care of things," he said.

Dave looked as cocky as a crowing rooster. "Don't fret," he replied. "Things'll be jim dandy when you get back. Just you bring home a mess of prime pelts, that's all I got to say."

Dave was grinning as though the whole thing were a big lark. And why not? He was staying in a snug cabin all winter while Jon was risking his neck going north to get furs for the money to pay their entrance fee. Just trust Dave to come out on top of every situation!

But the whole thing had been his own idea: the truth slapped his self-pity down where it should be. He had never thought leaving would be like this, sad and reluctantlike.

It wouldn't take much coaxing to make him call the whole thing off. But nobody seemed about to. He slapped Uriah gently on the seat of his pants and winked at Emma.

'See you all in the spring," he said as jauntily as he could manage; and without a backward glance, he took the reins of the horse, packed and ready, and walked away.

He wished it were Old Lightning instead of the sorry old nag he had bartered for in the village. But Dave wouldn't hear of his taking the family horse. "Think I'm going to pull that plow myself this spring?" his younger brother had demanded testily.

But he couldn't talk to this old horse. He wouldn't understand the way Old Lightning did.

At the far edge of the clearing back of the cabin he turned briefly and waved. Emma and Uriah stood in the doorway and waved back. So did Pa. Dave, by the woodpile, made a lazy arc with a piece of wood.

"Trying to make a big show of all the work he thinks he has to do this winter," Jon thought scornfully. "I just hope Ma and Emma don't do most of it to make it easy for him."

Jon walked on toward the spot along the creek bank where Old Josh had said he would meet him. Josh had slept in his cabin the night before, sharing it with the Liddicoats.

Jon switched his thoughts to the glowing face of Cindy when he had helped her and Pike move the family and their few household goods from the lean-to to the cabin.

His spirits rose a notch as he remembered her grateful whisper, "Likely Pa'll get well now."

"Likely he will," he'd replied, though his hopes had not been as high as hers. His own father hadn't got any better since he'd come back to a comfortable house and good food. Once the ager got hold of a body it never seemed to let go.

But it had done his heart good to see the Liddicoats in the snug cabin for the winter. And now that the Larkin danger was past, things would go a lot easier, too.

Everyone in the settlement agreed that they'd got just what they'd asked for. It should have been done long before, they said. And should be done to other ruffians along the river who made their living preying on boats and passengers, robbing and killing at will.

He passed the towering oak that stood on the corner of their land, the deep chip that Pa's blade had taken out still visible. That chip had been enough to mark the boundary when the Robertses had first arrived in the wilderness. Soon now it would take a government survey and payment of the entrance fee to register it at the land office to keep others from settling on it at will.

Early morning mists rose from the creek and swirled over the knobs. He passed the empty lean-to of the Liddicoats and felt better all over again thinking that Cindy and her family were no longer living in the sorry-looking thing. The animals had better shelters than that, he thought.

Pike's joy and relief at the sudden turn of events was a sight to behold. Hugging his old rifle to him, he beamed and said, "It'll be easy now getting enough for us to eat, and wood for the fire."

At first he had paled at hearing the fate of the Larkins; then he had acted like one coming out of a spell, or an animal unexpectedly released from a trap.

The neighbors seemed pleased, too, to see the Liddicoats moved. "First nice day of spring," Barkus promised, "we'll build 'em a cabin."

But where?

"My land'll be up for grabs in the spring," Old Josh said, " 'less'n I come back with enough furs to sell for the price of the entrance fee."

"Lot depends on this trip up north," Jon said soberly.

"Seems like." The old woodranger was not so concerned as the others, for he had only himself to worry about.

Jon's thoughts went again to Cindy. She had been on his mind a lot since yesterday. Seemed he couldn't shake off the memory of the warm, grateful glances she sent his way the minute she stepped inside Old Josh's cabin.

Purring like a kitten, she made her father comfortable by the fire. She straightened, looked about, and then up at Jon. The pinched look left her face, and she almost glowed with new hope and happiness. "A real cabin," she whispered, as though he had built it especially for her, "with a roof and log sides and a floor and a hearth."

She bounced and bustled about in a way that reminded Jon of his ma.

Jon pushed thoughts of both out of his mind. Good thing he was leaving with Old Josh. Few more days of this and he'd be mooning around like a lovesick swain, and his dream of living the life of a woodranger would go up in smoke.

Just like a woman, he thought scornfully, weaving webs about a man. Filmy they were, made up of soft words and shy glances, but once a man let himself be bound by them he found them as strong as deerhide thongs, wet and dried tight.

Jon straightened his shoulders and breathed deep of the cold, crisp air. Determinedly he thought of the months ahead with Old Josh. He'd be free of such ties, or know the reason why.

Josh was waiting at the appointed place on the creek bank where three willow trees grew, their long, feathery branches glittering with hoarfrost. The old man's breath and that of his horse hung suspended in the frosty air.

"Cabin too crowded," Old Josh said. "Glad to get out."

Jon nodded. "Know just how that is," he replied, and swallowed the last lump that had risen in his throat on his own leave-taking.

When the thin watery sun was directly overhead they reached the wide, hard-packed surface of the Buffalo Trace. Made by the huge animals on their way back and forth to the salt licks, it reached from Vincennes to the river at Jeffersonville. The Indians had used it for a trail, and now the settlers and travelers found it a good road from the former capital of the Territory to the new one at Corydon, not far from Jeffersonville.

They crossed the Trace, found the creek again, and kept to its banks. Reaching the spot where it forked into Indian Creek, they stopped to eat. Strips of boiled bear meat and a handful of parched corn were washed down with water from the stream.

After a few minutes' rest they went on. Old Josh found an Indian trail, now almost overgrown with underbrush, and followed it for some miles. It led to another twisting creek, which they followed for a short distance before plunging into the deep forest again.

The old man knew where he was going; Jon was content to lead the packhorses and look.

It was good land they were passing through. Poplar, beech, elm, ash, and honey locust trees grew straight and so tall in their quest for the sun that one could not see their tops. Their variety and size were proof the soil was rich beyond imagining. What a task to clear them off for plowing! But someday it would be done, Jon thought.

As the afternoon wore on Jon began to tire. His legs ached so, each mile seemed twice as long as the one before. Along with his mounting fatigue, the cold grew more penetrating.

Wouldn't Josh ever stop for the night? Fire, food—that was what Jon wanted now more than anything.

They came suddenly upon a wide path where trees lay uprooted, piled helter-skelter. It looked as though a huge scythe had cut a swath through the forest without purpose or meaning.

Jon stared amazed as they threaded their way across it.

Old Josh waved his hand. "Big wind," he said. "I seen one once, early spring. Got black and ugly, the sky did; then this pointed cloud come down a'roaring and tore up everything in its way. Turrible thing. I was glad it went back up 'fore it got to me." He squinted up the swath. "I recollect when fellers like us had to be mighty keerful goin' through one of these. Injuns like to hide in 'em."

Indians! Jon hadn't thought of them since they left that morning. With every step they were nearing Indian country. So far they hadn't seen one.

Darkness was closing in. In the distance Jon could hear the murmur of water over stones. From up ahead he heard Josh's muffled "It's the Muscatatuck. We'll stay the night here."

Jon could have shouted for joy.

"Know a place here dry as a bone," the old man said, and led the way to it.

Roots of a willow tree and earth and rocks jutted from a high bank of the Muscatatuck, forming a cave underneath.

It was dry, Jon noted, and sheltered on three sides from the wind, as well as from any intruders that might come. Slanting downward, the floor reached the creek some fifteen feet or so away.

"It's a sight better'n the Liddicoat hut," Jon grunted, and then wondered why that thought had come.

"Bin using it fer years," the old man said. "So've lots of others."

Bits of bone strewn about on the leaves blown in by the wind confirmed this.

"Hope nobody stops here tonight except us," Jon said, and he lugged the packs inside and laid them down on the leaves.

He tied the horses near a patch of brown winter grass, swept free of snow by the wind. The horses began to munch hungrily. Such grass was all the food they'd get to eat for months, and they seemed to know it.

Old Josh cleared the leaves from a shallow hole in front of the cave that was backed by a couple of flat stones. Jon gathered twigs and branches, which he broke over his knee. Soon a fire blazed there, sending light and warmth into the shadowy depths behind.

"Ain't no Injun danger round here," Josh said. "But there'll be other places we won't be so free to make a fire like this."

"I'm almighty glad we can have one tonight," Jon replied. They were squatting before the fire and soaking up the heat as they roasted pieces of raw bear meat on the ends of sticks.

On a flat stone between them lay a corn pone Ma had packed. It was close enough to the blaze to soak up some of the heat and would be warm when the meat was done.

Meat finally roasted, Jon broke the warm corn pone in two.

"Don't git vittles like this very often," the old man said, and he ate the bread with relish. "It takes womenfolks to bother with such like."

"No matter who made it," Jon said, munching a big piece, "it sure tastes mighty good."

The old man nodded. "We'll eat good while we kin," he said. "Soon enough we'll have to scrounge to fill our bellies. Rabbits and such kin sure make theirselves scarce when they think yer lookin' for 'em."

Jon, full as a tick, lay back content. The old man, as usual, was fretting when there was no cause to fret. There would always be something in the woods to eat that his trusty rifle could bring down. This was the life for a man, he thought— warm fire, full belly, nobody telling him to wipe off his feet.

As though reading his thoughts, the old man growled, "Up north small game gets scarce in winter."

Jon yawned. Old Josh sounded like Ma sometimes. Seemed to him she got real pleasure looking on the dark side of things. He supposed the old man was tired and he'd have to do the watching. Not that he thought there was anything to watch for.

Well, he was the young one of the two . . . if he could just stay awake. The fire . . . the food . . . He caught himself dozing and jerked up his head. With real effort he managed to open his eyes.

The old man's eyes gleamed with silent mirth. "Crawl in and sleep," he said, waving a gnarled hand at the cave. "I'll watch. Do my sleepin' with my eyes open, anyhow, when I'm on the trail."

➤Chapter-12➤

Jon awoke with a start. A horse whinnying inside the cabin loft? His eyes flew open. Dancing light patterns on the roof of the cave made him realize quickly enough where he was.

Why so bright a fire in the middle of the night? he wondered. Did Josh think a bear might try to claim their shelter for the night?

It was still night, wasn't it? Or was drowsiness muddling his thinking?

Jon lifted his head just enough so he could peer down the length of his blanket past his feet.

His toes almost touched Josh's back. The old man's grizzled head seemed bent over, as though he himself were dozing.

Some watch you are, Jon thought. An Injun could have sneaked in and scalped both of us, and you wouldn't have known the difference. Seems to me like you sleep with your eyes shut same as everybody else.

Injuns! Should they be more alert for them than this? Pa's warning came back. But Josh had said there wasn't much danger here, and he should know. Still . . . something made Jon stiffen with apprehension, made him want to see what was beyond Old Josh.

Slowly, soundlessly, Jon rose on one elbow, craned his neck so he could see over Josh's shoulder. The sight across the fire made his eyeballs freeze!

There, squatting on his haunches, eyes glittering like a snake's, was an Indian! Ugly broken teeth showed in an evil grin, heightened by the leaping lights and shadows that flitted across his earth-colored skin. Hooked nose, black hair hanging in greasy strands to his shoulders, added to the wild savagery of his looks.

Greed was there, too, and triumph. No wonder; he had trapped his quarry without any effort at all.

It came to Jon with a sickening thud that he and Old Josh were at the Indian's mercy. One move on their part and the Indian could snatch up the tomahawk lying beside him and fling it at either of them.

Still, there were two of them and only one Indian. Each of them had a rifle and a knife, and the tomahawk was the only weapon the Indian had, Jon thought cunningly.

If there were only some way of waking Josh, warning him of their danger, without the Indian knowing it. But nothing, no slight move, would escape those glittering eyes, Jon was sure.

Then his nose twitched. What was that smell—that tempting, tantalizing smell? Meat!

What in tunket . . . ? Jon raised his head just enough so he could once more peer over Josh's shoulder. The Indian saw him move—looked right at him—and grinned wider than ever!

Holding up a stick, the Indian brought the end of it to his long nose and sniffed loudly. Then he smacked his lips and cackled.

Jon fell back onto his leafy bed. Impaled on the end of the

stick was the carcass of a small animal, nicely browned and dripping!

For a moment Jon lay silent, though shaking as if with the ague. The Indian was cooking a meal while he calmly decided what to do with his white victims!

With an effort Jon quieted his quaking. This was no time to go to pieces; this was a time for cunning to match that of their savage foe. His rifle, primed and ready, stood leaning within arm's reach. One blast from it and there'd be one less Indian for the settlers to worry about. That is, if the Indian didn't get to his tomahawk first.

Jon's hand slid toward his rifle.

Another cackle from the Indian stopped him. It rattled back into the overhanging shelter and bounced about in an echo. Jon's head came up again and his gaze shot across the fire.

The Indian looked right at him, eyes glittering brightly. Up went the end of the stick again; and, with eyes on Jon, the Indian pointed to the animal cooking there.

"Rak-koon!" He cackled and smacked his lips and rubbed his stomach with his free hand.

Jon let his head fall back with a thud. That Indian had known all along he was awake. Indians were treacherous that way. You couldn't trust one farther than you could throw a barn by its door.

Then he heard a chuckle—from Old Josh. The trapper looked around, pointed to the roasting animal, and said, "Rak-koon good!"

The old man had known the Indian was there all along! Fear left Jon like wind through an open door. Whoever the Indian was, Josh wasn't afraid of him.

Jon sat up then. The Indian bobbed his head up and down,

pointed to the dripping meat on the stick, and cackled and babbled some more. Then both he and Old Josh howled in glee.

Jon touched Josh's shoulder. "What in tunket's so funny?" he demanded.

The old trapper turned, still chuckling, "He was saying how he sneaked up on that raccoon and hit it over the head with a stick."

Then, at Jon's wondering look, Josh added, "He's a Wea, wandered down south a ways. Weas are friendly Injuns, if you treat 'em right."

The Indian, sensing Josh was talking about him, bobbed his head up and down some more and uttered more unintelligible—to Jon—words.

Old Josh's eyes twinkled. "Says he seen our fire and hopes we don't mind his roasting his raccoon in it."

Jon let out a loud sigh of relief. "Lord, no," he said.

The Indian babbled on, all the while shaking an invisible substance over the roasting raccoon. Then he smacked his lips again.

"Wants to know if we got some salt," Josh translated. Then to their visitor he said, "Trade?"

The Indian nodded vigorously. He turned, reached behind him, and produced two fine-looking raccoon pelts.

Old Josh grinned at Jon. "Looks like we're starting our tradin' early. Them's good pelts, I kin see from here. But you go an' make a show of lookin' 'em over careful. We cain't let the Injuns think they kin cheat us."

Jon chuckled. Old Josh could joke when he'd a mind to. Walking around the fire, Jon realized the Indian's grin was foolish rather than evil, foolish and friendly. The glittering eyes now were trusting and eager, eager for salt. How right

Josh had been about bringing it for trade. "Next to whiskey, Indians like salt," the old man had said.

Jon picked up the skins and looked them over carefully, all the while feeling the beady eyes on him. They were on him as his fingers rubbed the fur back and forth to test its thickness and silkiness. These were prime skins, large and thick-furred. And they had been treated right. He looked toward Josh and nodded, then asked, "How much salt should I offer?"

" 'Bout a pint," the old trapper replied. "We ain't out to cheat him either."

Jon measured out a pint of salt. It had cost him the equivalent of a quarter of a raccoon skin, and not as good as these. He was making a good profit, and the Indian seemed delighted with the amount of salt he was receiving. Each was satisfied according to his needs.

The Indian held out a leather pouch and Jon poured the salt into it. It would season many a raccoon for him, the Indian seemed to say. Pleased, he offered some meat to Josh and Jon, but Josh said, "We got plenty," with a shake of his head.

The Indian grinned again, and then ate the meat off the stick in big, tearing bites. Finished, he rose, and as silently as he had appeared, disappeared into the night.

Old Josh, peering into the darkness after him, said to Jon, " 'Pears like that Wea is going to get his wish."

"What wish?" Jon yawned, wishing that he could go back into the cave and sleep some more. But it was Josh's turn to sleep now.

"He wished it would snow hard and turn colder. Says that's the only good weather for raccoon and muskrat hunts."

Jon already knew that, so he said nothing as he squatted

down and poked at the fire before throwing on two more pieces of wood.

Old Josh went into the cave, and Jon could hear the old man's bones crack as he crawled into his blanket.

"I'm all right," he replied to Jon's inquiring glance. "Jest a touch of the rheumatiz. Long's I keep movin' it don't bother me much." He yawned loudly. "It's when I stop I get in trouble. Takes me a while to get goin' in the mornin' this kind of weather."

Jon's self-esteem rose, filled him with an odd kind of satisfaction. Yesterday the old man had the edge on him, going, going, until it seemed Jon's legs would drop off. Now he knew it hadn't been an abundance of vigor on the old man's part, but only that he'd been forcing himself to go on. Come morning, Jon's youthful muscles would be ready and raring to go, but the old man's would need priming like a pump.

His blanket wrapped around his shoulders, Jon sat before the fire until dawn. Once in a while he rose and went out for more fuel, to look at the horses, and to take a look around their camp. Then, wrapped in his blanket, he threw wood on the blaze whenever it died down, and tried his best to keep awake. But doze he did, though he hoped Josh didn't notice.

The warmth of the fire seemed to thin out as morning approached, no matter how much wood he put on it. It was getting colder all right, just as the Wea had hoped it would. By daybreak the wind was whipping icy pellets of half snow and half sleet into the shelter.

Their breakfast, a handful each of parched corn, did nothing to warm Jon up either. A bowl of warm porridge would taste mighty good, he ventured to remark. But Old Josh had ruled that one warm meal a day was enough for men on the move.

"Well, I'll be!" Josh exclaimed, as they sat chewing on the dry corn that stuck in Jon's throat. "News sure travels fast."

Jon peered up through the sleety sheet coming down on the other side of their sputtering fire. Three Indians—a man, a woman, and a boy—were approaching their camp. And all of them carried pelts.

"More Weas," the old man said, and rose to greet them in their own tongue. Jon marveled at Josh's understanding and speaking a language that, to Jon, sounded like rocks pouring down a hillside.

The Indians halted; the man stepped forward, hand raised in greeting. "Trade," he grunted in English.

Then he jabbered some more in his own tongue, and Old Josh jabbered back. Finished, the old man turned to Jon.

"Says he heard white men on creek have salt to trade." He grinned. "They got tobacco too?"

"You bet they have," Jon replied with enthusiasm.

This trading business, he thought, was going to be as easy as eating one of Ma's squash pies. It was strange how his mind was so much on food this morning! At this rate they'd soon have all the pelts they could pack in the dugout on their trip back to New Albany.

"The Indians'll be glad to trade a good dugout for these two old horses," Old Josh had said. "It'll be a sight easier and faster coming back on the rivers than going up will be."

This morning Jon felt he couldn't get back home too soon.

The Indians showed eight excellent muskrat skins. Old Josh traded a twist of tobacco for four of them, and Jon traded a pint and a half of salt for the others.

The Indian woman, beaming her pleasure at the salt, produced a wooden bowl from beneath the blanket wrapped about her. Steam still rose from its contents.

John sniffed. Whatever the bowl held, it was warm, and it smelled good.

"Take it," Josh told him. "It'll make 'em mad if you don't." Jon took the bowl, smiled his thanks, and the Indians left.

Old Josh watched them go. "We're close to a Wea village," he said. He bent over and sniffed the contents of the bowl in Jon's hand. "Dried corn," he said, "cooked with dried berries and nuts. Smells right tasty."

"It does that," Jon agreed, the smell still rising and tantalizing his nostrils.

"Then eat," old Josh ordered. "Young stummicks kin hold more'n old ones kin."

Greedily Jon scooped out the thick mush with his fingers. He wiped the bowl as clean as if Emma had washed it.

"Fine a meal as I ever had in my life," he said. "What will I do with this bowl?" He looked it over. "Carved from the burl of an oak," he said admiringly, "and polished as slick as any Dave ever made. We cain't carry it, and it seems a shame to throw it away."

Old Josh was tying the last pack on their horses.

"Leave it right there," he said, pointing to the cave. "That's where that squaw will expect to find it when she comes fer it. Likely it's her best bowl and she wouldn't want to lose it."

Jon set the bowl carefully where it could be easily seen. Then, feeling much better with his stomach full, he followed Old Josh. They found a shallow place to ford the creek and continued on their way.

"I thought you said we had to be mighty keerful with the Injuns," he said to Josh. "Those Weas didn't seem to need watching." Old Josh said sharply, "They's good Injuns and bad ones, same as whites. All we meet won't be as easy to get along with as them Weas."

➤Chapter-13➤

They spent that night in a bark hut Josh had built on his way north the year before. It was plain that others had used it for shelter since then, as remnants of fires and bones were strewn about the dirt floor.

"Injuns likely," Old Josh grunted as they let their packs slip to the floor. "I've used many a one they built."

Once inside, with a fire going before the open side, it was as comfortable as the cave had been.

"Wonder if any Injuns'll be by tonight," Jon said, throwing another stick onto the blaze. "Wouldn't mind a bit to do some more trading."

Old Josh shook his head as he stuck some bear meat onto the end of a stick for roasting. It was the last of the food they had brought along, so they knew they'd have to forage the next day.

"No Wea villages around here I recollect of," the old woodranger said, holding the chunk of meat so the flames licked around it. "But soon's we git across the White River we'll run into the Delawares. They's fourteen of their villages strung out along the Wapihani, as they call the river. Outain-

107

ink, or Old Town, is the one we'll hit. Likely we'll do some tradin' there."

Jon slept well that night, stomach full, body warm, and mind swarming with all the fine pelts coming his way so easily.

A freezing rain was falling when they reached the Wapi-hani several days later.

Jon stared in dismay at the swirling waters, only a scant two inches below the riverbanks. Swollen by fall rains, the current was swift; churning by were limbs and logs and whole trees, with twisted roots that looked as though they had been ripped loose by the current's tug and pull.

"This'n is a lot too deep and wide and wild to ford," he mumbled through lips stiffened with cold.

Old Josh grinned faintly, his skin seeming to crack. "Don't fret," he said. "An Injun'll see us and figure he kin take us across in his canoe and make hisself some money or trade goods."

Jon exhaled slowly. "Take a canoe across in this?" he asked in amazement. He was wet to the skin and shivering cold and wanted more than anything to believe Old Josh was right. But one look at those raging waters convinced him the old man was addled in the head.

Josh nodded, small icicles on his fur cap and the ends of his long hair and beard crackling.

"I seen 'em cross in worse'n this." Squinting, he peered off into the gray wetness.

Jon's gloom only deepened. The old man was more than addled; he was crazy. And so was he, Jon, for ever coming with him. He'd be a sight better off if he'd stayed home. Right now Dave was likely sitting close to the fire, warming his toes and cracking nuts and eating them. And the wood that warmed him probably cut by Ma and Emma.

Anger rose in Jon. That dratted Dave! Ever since he'd been knee-high to a grasshopper Dave had had things easy. While he, Jon . . .

"Here comes one now!" Old Josh shouted.

Sure enough a young Indian appeared through the sheet of sleet. He stopped before them, scowling, and waved his hand at the horses and packs and the two men, and then at the river.

Old Josh seemed to waver. Jon could have kicked his hindsides. Here was their deliverance, and the old man hesitated!

The old man gabbled something, eyes narrowed. Now what was he saying to that Indian? A small doubt rose in Jon's mind. He wished he knew more about Old Josh, besides the fact that he was part Indian himself.

The young Indian snapped an answer. Josh hesitated again. Then he nodded and, turning to Jon, said, "Says he'll take us across for a dollar."

Jon's trading instinct came to the fore then. "How about salt?" Dollars were what he had to have for that entrance fee; the government was not in the fur business.

Old Josh shook his head. "Save that fer tradin'," he said. "These Delawares'll likely have some fine furs."

"Then a dollar it is," Jon said, and nodded too.

From some bushes, the Indian brought out a canoe.

"We'll take the packs first," Old Josh said. "He'll come back for you and the horses."

In no time the old man, the Indian, and the packs were in the canoe and shoving off. As the Indian set the paddle firmly into the swirling waters, Jon felt a sudden emptiness in his stomach.

Why in the name of common sense had he agreed to this? Here he was left with two old horses while Old Josh and that

Indian made off with all the trade goods and everything else Jon owned except his rifle!

For one who had warned Jon about them, Old Josh seemed mighty familiar with the Indians. There was nothing now to stop the old woodranger from keeping those goods and reaping all the profits for himself!

Panic rose in Jon. The canoe had disappeared into the mists that swirled over the murky waters—canoe, Indian, Josh, everything! Maybe there was an Indian village over there and maybe there wasn't!

What an addlepated idiot he was. Indians were as tricky as cornered animals and, like the animals, would fight back any way they could. Old Josh was as much Indian as white man. And the Indians had been cornered at the treaty of Greenville a couple of years before!

"They're madder'n hornets at the white men for taking their hunting grounds away from 'em," Jon had heard more than once. "They think they were cheated, and maybe they were."

And he had walked right into a trap set by them. Likely Old Josh and that Indian were laughing theirselves sick right now.

Well, maybe not right now. The mists parted for an instant, and Jon saw the canoe; the Indian seemed to be having trouble. He'd been swept downstream a ways and was fighting to keep from being turned about by the swirling current.

Jon's heart was in his throat. Several times it seemed that the frail canoe would lose its battle with the raging river. He feared for the men's safety. Helplessly, he watched and wondered if canoe, goods, and men would be swept under.

How could it be otherwise? Hugging his rifle close under his deerskin coat, Jon inwardly strained to help the Indian

110

keep his craft under control. He made every movement the red man did.

Suddenly, to his intense relief, he saw the canoe shoot toward the opposite bank, as though in one mighty effort it had freed itself from a whirlpool.

A feather of mist obscured it again, and then was swept away. Jon could just barely make out several Indians running toward the bank. Eagerly they grabbed hold of the canoe and pulled it to safety.

"Whew!" Jon let out a long, low whistle of relief. He turned and hugged the horse's neck. "They got across!"

Then the doubts returned. Would the Indian risk his neck coming back for him? That is, if he had meant to in the first place?

Jon tried to see across the waters. Minutes had passed and dusk was settling. Through the darkness and the mist he could see only a short distance. But he could hear the snakelike swish of the wicked, swirling waters. Then through the mist he saw a speck. The speck grew larger. Glory be! Jon felt like shouting at the top of his lungs. It was the canoe and the Indian! Coming back!

How could he have ever doubted the loyalty of his old friend? He had little time for self-castigation, though; for sooner than he thought possible, the canoe was on his side of the river again.

The Indian grinned at him faintly, as if he knew what Jon had been thinking. Jon grinned back. A sort of empathy sprang up between them. They were about the same age and not so different as one might think.

"Hold horse rein," the Indian said. "Horses swim."

Jon bridled at the patronizing tone of the Indian's voice. Did he think Jon had expected to put the horses in the canoe?

111

Still, this was no time for him to fly off the handle. This wasn't Ma or Dave or Emma, who would overlook his display of temper. This Indian could leave him right where he was.

Meekly Jon got into the canoe, holding the reins of the horses. The animals protested at entering the swirling, icy water. But after some tugging they did. As they swam alongside they seemed to hold the course of the canoe steadier. Without incident they got across, and men and horses walked up the other bank of the river.

Old Josh greeted them. Then he turned to a solemn, hatchet-faced old Indian standing apart from the crowd that had gathered. The old Indian looked regal and proud in spite of the tattered blanket wrapped about his shoulders.

"Lapihani," Old Josh introduced him to Jon, "Big Bear, chief of the village. Says he wants us to stay the night in their long house. I told him we'd be mighty proud to." The old man lowered his voice. "It'll be warm and dry; and he says the braves were lucky and brought back deer meat, so we'll have plenty to eat."

Food! Jon was tired and hungry. He would have spent the night with a bear if a warm bed and food were included.

"I'm more'n willing to stay," he said thankfully.

Outainink, he could see, was a small village of eight wigwams. But Big Bear walked as proudly and solemnly as if there were eighty. Motioning them to follow, the chief led them to the long house set high on the riverbank.

"Big Bear says dance and feast this evening," Old Josh said as they climbed the hill. "A fat deer or two brought back by braves, and they make big over it."

"That's reason enough for me, too," Jon said. White men did the same, he reflected, using any excuse to feast and dance, from log raising to husking bee. Still, as they neared the long

112

house he thought, bunch of Indians get two white men in there and anything can happen. Wind up with tomahawks in their backs, likely as not.

Smoke boiled out of three holes in the roof of the long low building of split logs. The smell of roasting meat assailed his nostrils. Jon drooled and forgot his fears. His eyes took in the chattering children, two laughing women, and another old man who walked with Lapihani. How could he feel afraid of them?

But as he walked into the murky darkness inside the long house his heart skipped a beat and he swallowed hard. Fear formed a hard knot in his chest as he looked around.

Along the sides of the building ran a sort of bench, about a foot high and five feet wide. It was made of dirt scooped up and packed hard and covered with grass. Indian men sat on it, eating from bowls tendered them by one of the squaws.

Black, beady eyes turned on the newcomers, full of suspicion and, Jon was certain, hate. The knot in his chest grew larger and made his breathing painful.

Old Josh and Big Bear seemed friendly—too friendly maybe. How did he know they hadn't planned all this, get him in here and kill him and take his horse and trade goods? Indians as poor as these would think his supply of salt well worth a killing or two. And Old Josh would profit from his horse and other goods.

All the warnings he had heard came flooding back to him during the few seconds it took him to be seated on the bench beside Old Josh. He couldn't show his fear. He had to look as unconcerned as a raccoon on a floating log.

A squaw brought them bread of corn baked in flat cakes. Another handed each a wooden bowl of deer-meat stew.

Jon tried to down his fears. But he almost jumped out of

his skin as he felt someone sit down beside him, so close he felt a thigh against his own.

Jon turned his head quickly, to find himself looking into the eyes of the Indian who had ferried him across the river.

"Me Malk'wa-tut," the lad said solemnly, adding, "Little Bear."

"Big Bear's son?"

The Indian grunted, and pointing to the bowl in Jon's hand, he grinned. "Good?"

Jon's head went up and down. "Sure is," he said, and took a big bite of the corn cake. Somehow he felt at ease with Little Bear.

An Indian squaw gave Little Bear a bowl of stew and some cakes. As they ate the boys kept glancing at each other, uttering a word now and then that they thought was understood.

With each glance Jon noticed the jacket Little Bear was wearing, and his admiration of it grew. It was soft and white, made of deerskin, as only the Indians could make it, and the sleeves were of prime beaver. Jon had never seen anything so handsome in his whole life.

Little Bear, aware of the admiring glances, preened like a fine-feathered male bird. "Good, huh?" He grinned and touched his jacket with a finger.

"Purtiest thing I ever saw," Jon replied, running a finger down one soft sleeve.

Little Bear sat up even straighter, pride fairly quivering within him.

An unaccustomed feeling of envy rose in Jon. How he wished he owned that jacket!

He had to have it! And he would have it, too, before he left this village. An Indian would trade anything he owned.

But should he trade his precious goods for something for himself?

He had come up here to get furs to sell for cash money with which to pay the entrance fee on their land. A fur jacket on his own back, no matter how handsome, would not impress the man at the land office.

Jon fought down the desire. Deliberately he turned his eyes away so as not to see it any more than he had to. It was then he noticed the sharp contrast between Little Bear's handsome jacket and the older men's shabby buckskins and tattered white man's blankets.

"They sure look down in the mouth," he said to Josh. "Don't look like they're celebratin' anything to me."

"They always look so," Old Josh replied. "They been beat and chased outen everwhere they've lived. They used to live on the Delaware River eastward, but the Iroquois and the whites druv 'em here. Now they know it's only a matter of time 'fore they got to move agin." The old man shook his head and took another slurping swallow of stew. "Seems a shame. Never was a fightin' bunch, the Leni-Lenape, just friendly and peace-lovin'. But they don't find peace, no matter where they go."

There went Old Josh again, Jon thought, siding with the Indians. One minute he warned against them, and the next he praised and felt sorry for them. Were they to be feared or pitied? Jon decided he'd never find out from Josh.

Soon several young braves entered the long house. They didn't look beaten like the old men. Instead they laughed and chatted and looked full of cheer, as though life, even in defeat, could be good.

The young braves danced about the fire, whooping and yelling in high spirits. Then they sat down to eat.

Lapihani rose, clutching his tattered blanket tightly about him. How much finer was the jacket of his son, Jon thought. Again the desire to have the jacket surged through him.

But it was forgotten as he listened to Lapihani speak. His eyes on Jon and Old Josh, the chief of the village said, "We, poor tribe of the once-great Leni-Lenape, welcome our guests. Eat and rest with us."

The glittering black eyes then swept around the room. "For our guests," the old man continued, "we will read the Wa'lum O'lum of our people." He looked again at Jon and Josh. "White man call it our Talking Wood."

➤Chapter-14➤

An old man limped into the long house. Tenderly and reverently he carried a bundle wrapped in snow-white deerskin. With great solemnity he laid it on the ground before Lapihani.

An awed hush fell over the onlookers. Old Josh whispered to Jon, "They only do this at special times. I reckon they think our bein' here is one."

Jon looked around, noting the solemn, expectant looks on the faces of the older men and the quiet mien of the young braves.

"Just like when Pa gets out the Bible to read," he whispered back.

"This *is* their Bible."

The limping one unrolled the bundle. There, ranged in a neat row on the deerskin, were five stacks of thin boards. By craning his neck Jon could see that pictures were painted on each board.

Little Bear noted his interest and whispered, "They tell the story of my people." Then he added, with a nod toward the man who had carried them in, "Broken Arrow only one in our village can read them now."

Was it bitterness in his voice that this was so? Or relief that times were changing?

The faint beat of a drum rolled through the long house. Broken Arrow stood, arms folded and head held high. Eyes staring straight ahead, he waited until the last note had died away. Then he picked up the top board of the stack at his left hand. Looking down at it, he began to chant.

The rhythm of the chant, half song with overtones of sadness, made Jon think of Ma singing the old love ballads. They, too, told of things that once were and were no more.

Old Josh and Little Bear joined in telling Jon the meaning of the chant. As he listened Jon had the queer feeling he had heard part of the story before.

The first board told of a time long ago when there was no world at all. Kee-shay-la-muh'ka-ong, the Creator, brought one into being, but it was destroyed by a flood caused by an evil monster.

Broken Arrow paused a moment before picking up the second board. Then he resumed his chant, and Old Josh explained its meaning to Jon, with Little Bear nodding in agreement.

"Then came the powerful brave Nanabush," the chant said, "and he created another world, the one in which we live now. But the evil monster turned himself into the great snake, Man-it'to, and flooded it again. The Leni-Lenape, the Real People, escaped together to a huge island, which they found was really a giant turtle."

Jon couldn't help it. He had to grin as he thought of people riding the back of a turtle. But the grin disappeared as he saw Little Bear frowning at him. Well, he wouldn't want anyone to laugh at any of the stories of the Bible either.

"The turtle began to swim," the story went on, "and the

Leni-Lenape went with it. The land to which the turtle first took them was cold, and there was snow all the time. So some of the Leni-Lenape moved southward. On the way, they fought with other tribes and divided into many groups themselves. They settled along the seacoast of a great land. Here they found a strange plant with ears of grain, which we call maize, and which tasted very good. Soon they learned to raise this grain, and they were joyful that they now had something to eat besides the flesh of fish and animals and the roots and barks and berries and nuts they found in the woods. They were joyful now they had a good food, the planting and harvesting and storing of which they could control themselves."

Jon sat and listened and learned of many great chiefs of the Leni-Lenape, and of their deeds. He heard of the coming of the white men in their great winged canoes, and of the terrible warlike Iroquois, who appeared out of the north and conquered the Lenape again and again. He heard about their westward trek to a place where they hoped there would be no warlike enemies and plenty of land where they could raise corn. This they found in the great Ohio valley. And there they stayed until the white man came and defeated them, and they knew at last they would have to move on again.

The last stick read, Broken Arrow wrapped them all carefully in the deerskin and limped silently out of the long house.

Awestruck and solemn now himself, Jon sat and watched Chief Lapihani rise. Looking straight ahead, chin high and blanket around him, the old chief said, "We who are old continue to hope the telling of the Wa'lum O'lum will help our young people remember how good were the ancient ways of our people and make them want to return to them."

The young braves were quiet and thoughtful, drawn

119

into a mood of reverence for the age-old story. But only for a little while. As soon as Lapihani and some of the older men had left, the young men became boisterous again. It was today they meant to enjoy, not the past. They crowded around Old Josh and Jon, and made signs and spoke the few words of English they knew to tell the newcomers they had furs to trade for the white man's goods.

Next morning the world outside the long house was covered with a glaze of ice. The trees snapped and crackled in their brittle coats, and even the Indians slipped and slid to keep right side up as, with furs on arms, they came to trade. Old Josh and Jon spread out their wares and made ready to trade with the Delawares.

Little Bear appeared with six fine beaver skins. Again he wore the fine jacket.

Suddenly Jon asked, "Trade?" and put one finger on the soft fur of one sleeve.

Little Bear drew himself up proudly. He swept one arm toward the goods of the white men, as though to tell them they did not have enough to make him part with his handsome possession. "No trade," he snapped.

In spite of his disappointment, Jon felt a surge of pleasure. It was good to see his friend lift his head in pride. He was also glad he had not traded his goods off for something just for himself. "That entrance fee on our land is much more important," he told himself firmly.

Early next morning Josh poked Jon in the ribs. "Best git goin'," he said. "Footin' outside ain't bad this morning." As Jon sat up and yawned lustily, the old man added, "We don't want to wear out our welcome here at Outainink."

Jon slid off the bunk in the long house, went to the door, and peered out.

"More snow last night," he said, rubbing his eyes to rid them of their heavy sleepiness. "Right smart, too."

The old man stood beside him and mused, "Just enough to cover the slipperiness. Ought to make good time on it. Best kind o' huntin' and trappin' weather there is."

"Yep, it sure is," Jon agreed cheerfully.

Things had gone well for him the day before. He had a bundle of fine beaver and marten skins that would bring good prices in the spring. There were some coonskins in his bundle, too, along with two red fox furs and four deerskins, as soft as smoke and as pliable as velvet.

These he figured to trade off in Fort Wayne for more trade goods.

"They's a silversmith there," Old Josh told him, "that makes buckles and such that the Indians like most as well as whiskey. I take along a few of 'em 'cause they get so much pride out o' deckin' theirselves out in 'em. They don't harm 'em none, and they git their skins' worth."

A grin of satisfaction spread over Jon's face as he turned back into the long house. In his pack was a pair of moccasins that Little Bear's mother had made and traded for salt. They were decorated with embroidery of quill and beads that another white man had traded them. Jon had thought of Cindy when he'd made the trade. They'd look a sight different on her feet than the rags she wore around them.

Reaching over to pick up his bundle of pelts, he saw the small white oval of her face. The big black eyes smiled at him, as if in thanks for his gift of the moccasins.

"Hmph," he snorted. More likely she'd blaze up mad and tell him she didn't want charity from him or anybody else. Serve him right, too, for going all soft and silly and trading that salt for a pair of pretties for her. Such thoughts would only end up in a wedding and a houseful of young 'uns and the end of the free life he was leading right now. Instead of hunting and trading, he'd be pulling stumps and plowing.

"What say?" Old Josh said as Jon snorted again.

"I said this ka-ha-ma'kun that Little Bear's Ma gave me would taste mighty good on the trail," Jon replied as he started outside with his bundle of furs.

"It shore will," Old Josh agreed. "Mixed with hot water and tree sugar it will eat real fine."

Packed and on their way, they later crossed a great open meadow, as smooth and flat as a cabin floor. Fording a small creek on the other side, they plunged into another forest. Jon sorted out white oak, walnut, elm, sycamore, and honey locust, grown so tall it seemed forty feet up before a single limb appeared on their trunks.

Only fine land could produce such trees—rich land! Jon snorted again. Here he was, thinking like a farmer.

The next sight was more to his liking. In the ice-encrusted center of a small lake a number of dome-shaped mud and stick beaver houses could be seen. The sharp flap of a beaver tail told them activity was going on in the waters beneath the ice and inside the snow-topped houses.

"Maybe we should stop and set traps," Jon suggested.

Old Josh shook his head. "On the move ain't no time to stretch and cure skins," he said. "Best do that some place we plan to stop a few days. Trappin's a sight better farther north."

Another creek ahead was narrow but deep, and the current was unexpectedly swift. The horses floundered, and Jon and the old woodranger waded in icy waters up to their thighs.

Minutes after Jon got out of the water his deerskin breeches were as stiff and icy as the water had been.

"That's why the Injuns like the white man's wool cloth," Old Josh said. "And they like cotton calico for summer, too. Wool's a sight warmer in winter, and cotton's cooler in summer than any skin kin be. I guess that's why young Injuns will keep leanin' toward white man's ways. They's just better'n old Injun ways."

In spite of his discomfort, Jon chuckled. "And now we're out for the skins they don't want, to sell to the white man to wear. Don't make much sense, seems to me."

He wished his breeches were made of good wool strouding, instead of the frigid armor encasing his legs right now. But Ma's sheep hadn't produced enough wool for all their needs, and the strouding he had bought was for trading to the Indians for more skins. The whole thing struck him as ironical.

"Beaver skins are made into hats," Old Josh reminded him. "Seems a man acrost the ocean don't think he's amounted to much 'less'n he owns a beaver hat. An' the other furs are used fer coats and the like, and deerskins are made into pouches an' gloves." He slapped his own deerskin-covered thigh and it crackled. "They don't use 'em fer britches."

"Then they use good sense," said Jon.

They camped that night beneath an overhanging rock on the bank of another small stream. It made a fine windbreak, and they settled down to a warm and comfortable rest behind the other screen of their fire.

It had been better in the Delaware long house, though, Jon thought as he filled his belly with the ka-ha-ma'kun fixed as Josh had told him, but without the tree sugar. The corn pudding tasted good anyhow, along with pieces of roasted deer meat the Delawares had given them.

It was Josh's turn to keep watch again. Jon hoped the old

man didn't doze off, as he didn't want to miss any Indians he might trade with, and said so. Old Josh sharply reminded him they could also run into some Indians that didn't have trading in mind.

Jon just grinned and went off to sleep. That kind of talk was just a lot of old-woman gabbling; he was sure of it now.

He was awakened by a shrill, blood-curdling whoop that seemed to come from very near. Jerking himself upright, he saw Old Josh sitting behind the fire, rifle ready.

"Injuns, all right," the old man muttered without turning his head. "And mebbe not so friendly as the Weas and the Delawares."

To Jon's surprise the old woodranger gave a low whoop in return. Into the glow of the campfire there quickly stepped a single Indian.

Fear crept up Jon's spine and prickled the back of his neck. Those shifty, glittering eyes peering across the glow of the fire were anything but friendly. A long hooked nose set between them, the tip almost overhanging a twisted snaggle-toothed mouth. From the darkness into the light of the fire now stepped a woman, as meanly dressed as her man, but with a hang-dog, rather than an evil, look on her dirty face.

The Indian saw the chunk of deer meat that hung on a pole where it would be safe from marauding animals. With a grunt he bent the pole toward him and took the meat off the end.

Jon eyed Old Josh. Would the woodranger protest such gall on the Indian's part? The answer was no. The faded old eyes just kept a wary watch while the Indian picked up Jon's knife and hacked off a piece of the frozen meat. Then he put it on the end of a stick and thrust it into the fire.

The woman watched hungrily as the meat sputtered and

124

sizzled in the flames. Still she hung back, as though afraid to come closer to the warmth, the meat, or her man.

Meat hardly thawed, the Indian began gnawing on it like a half-starved animal. Jon would have grabbed his knife to prevent the Indian from hacking off more, but Old Josh stopped him with a warning look.

"Let him git his own meat," Jon said indignantly.

"He's got no bow and arrow or knife," Old Josh said in a half whisper.

So that was why the Indian had looked so queer. No Indian would appear so outside his village, unless there was a reason. What could it be?

The old man slowly moved his head from side to side. Best wait and see, the silent motion said plainly.

The Indian woman stayed a respectful distance from her companion, yet all the while her own beady eyes were on him enviously as he ate. After his second chunk of meat the Indian gave a loud belch, rubbed his stomach, and waved the woman closer.

He grunted something, then cut off a piece of the meat and tossed it at her feet. Then, still holding Jon's knife, he stretched out beside the fire and started to snore loudly.

Old Josh turned toward Jon, then, and said softly, "Renegade from some tribe. Potawatomi, looks like. They're mean Indians when riled. This'n got kicked out in a hurry for some deviltry, or he'd have some kind of weapon. Best to string along with 'em. No sense pickin' a fight with an Indian 'less'n there's a better reason than a piece o' meat." The old man continued to sit, rifle in hand. "Sech Indians as these is like dealin' with a nest o' snakes. Better to go around than stir 'em up."

Josh indicated that that was just what he intended doing.

Well, Jon might as well do the same thing. He lay back on his twig bed and closed his eyes.

A sound no louder than a squirrel leap caused him to open his eyes, raise his head, and look. His heart popped twice its size.

The old fool! The stupid old fool! To turn his back to that Indian for even a fleeting second. Now the Indian, holding high Jon's hunting knife, was rising, ready to plunge the blade into the old woodranger's back.

Jon felt the woman's eyes on him. One move and she would warn the man, and that knife would come Jon's way, point first.

But he had to do something. With Old Josh gone, he'd be no match for those two. They'd wind up with everything.

It was risky, but he had to try. Summoning all his strength, Jon began to roll over and over toward the Indian's legs. The woman shrieked, and the Indian turned, but too late. Jon's body rolled close; his arms seized the dirty legs, and the Indian fell, his face in the red-hot coals of the fire's rim.

Shrieks of anguish filled the frosty air as the knife flew out of his hand and landed at Old Josh's feet. Josh picked it up and Jon relaxed his grip.

Holding his face and still moaning, the Indian staggered off into the darkness, the woman close on his heels.

"They ain't apt to come back," Old Josh said.

"It was right foolish of you to turn your back on that Indian," Jon said reprovingly.

Old Josh handed Jon his knife. "And it was right foolish of you," he said, "to leave that knife where he could pick it up so handy."

➤Chapter-15➤

Days later Josh and Jon made camp outside the palisades of Fort Wayne. Nestled in a clearing along the bank of the St. Mary's, where it joined the St. Joseph to become the Maumee, the fort was a scene of hustle and bustle. Indians, trappers, and traders trotted back and forth, from the forests on foot, and upstream and downstream in the canoes and pirogues that lined the riverbank.

"What a fair sight that is!" Jon cried, coming out of the bark hut they had hastily erected at the edge of the clearing. Leaning on his rifle, he looked down toward the fort and the river.

"Wal, I wouldn't say it was pretty," Old Josh growled. "Jest an overgrowed log cabin with a couple o' blockhouses, and soldiers struttin' around."

Jon made no reply. It wasn't the fort he was thinking about, or the muddy rutted paths, or the slushy fields and houses spreading out in front of him. It was the people, those two-legged humans moving about. He had got almighty tired of Old Josh's company, if he'd told the truth of it.

Oh, he and the old woodranger had got along amiably

127

enough on the long trek north. But having been accustomed all his life to neighbors, going to New Albany with corn to grind or to trade, and living in the warm, albeit sometimes annoying, circle of his family, the trip had seemed mighty lonely toward the end.

They had met other Indians, some friendly and some not. All had been willing to trade furs for salt and strouding and such. But that wasn't the same as meeting others of his own kind.

They would be here in the vicinity of the fort for a few days. "We'll git supplies and more trade goods, and then move on and set up winter camp," Josh said. "And we'll let the commandant here know we're about, so if we come up missin' he'll send some of them purty soldiers to look for us, mebbe."

His opinion of the soldiery wasn't very high, so Jon learned.

Soon he and Old Josh were on their way to the fort, each carrying a bundle of the furs they had collected on the way up.

"Now jest watch me," the old man advised Jon. "I'll show ye how to deal with these traders so's ye git the most fer yer furs. They'll cheat ye outen yer eyeteeth ef'n ye ain't keerful, and it don't make no difference if yer skin is red or white." He shook his head. "Fur tradin's a scrabblin', rascally business, even at best, with the trapper allus comin' out the little end of the horn."

Jon decided he'd learn all he could from Josh. In some ways it didn't seem the old man was smart enough to come in out of the rain, but when it came to trading he had already shown his shrewdness. Jon didn't want to go through all this and then lose out on what he came for. If he did, he'd never hear the last of it—from Dave, anyhow. And he did want to show that dratted Dave a thing or two.

"We'll leave some of our best 'uns here for another day o' tradin'," Old Josh said as they left the hut.

"Won't somebody steal 'em?" Jon asked.

"Ain't much o' that goes on up here." Josh spat. "Penalty fer fur stealin' comes purty high." He didn't elaborate on it; he didn't have to. Jon realized that the trappers must have their own way of dealing with such, same as the settlers farther south. Likely they weren't so slow meting out the punishment either.

"This is one o' the busy seasons o' the year," Josh said as they walked along. "T'other one's spring. Both are times fer the trappers to come in and blow their six months' work on reg'lar whingdings o' drinkin' and carousin', jest hoping they have stake enough left to git trade goods and grub to last till next time."

"Thought they didn't sell whiskey around the fort."

"They don't. But acrost the river is a town o' Frenchies, and they do."

A raucous yell and a shot sounded from across the canoe- and pirogue-filled river.

"Over there," Josh pointed to the opposite bank of the river, "is Miami Town. Not so many Indians there as used t' be when it was the main town of the Miamis. Called it Kekionga then. Right powerful tribe in their day, the Miamis."

Old Josh said "howdy" to a bewhiskered, rough-looking white man who staggered past. He was a trapper: that was plain.

Jon looked back over his shoulder at the sodden wreck of

a man. "Don't any of them ever hang onto their cash money, and leave?" he asked.

"Not many," Josh replied. "Lot of 'em runnin' away from somethin' when they come here. Some of 'em stay because they like the way they're livin'. Others jest don't have anywhere to go back to."

A sorry lot, Jon thought, as he passed them coming and going. Some were Indians; some were white; and some, half-breeds like Old Josh. Dirty buckskins hanging in shreds, mottled faces covered with beards; the young swaggered, but the old ones shuffled and peered out at the world through eyes bloodshot with drink.

Old Josh regarded Jon beadily. "As I said, the fur trade is a rascally, scrabbly business, 'ceptin' fer the big guns ownin' the fur comp'nies. I ain't never seen a trapper have more'n enough to last his next time to the fort."

"Then why . . . ?"

"I never had brains enough to quit," Old Josh snarled. "Anyway, there's one thing trappin' does fer a man, and that's spile him fer any other kind o' work."

An aged Indian went by, wrapped in a bright blanket and carrying an iron cooking kettle hugged tightly to his breast.

"He's thinkin' of all the tasty stews his squaw'll make in that pot." Old Josh grinned. "Iron is a sight better than clay, and the Injuns caught on to that right quick."

A squealing pig caught Jon in the back of the legs and almost toppled him. It was followed by a howling dog.

The gate of the fort was open. A uniformed soldier stepped from inside the palisade.

"Halt!" he said, his smooth-shaven, boyish face sternly set.

"Not much older'n I am," Jon thought. And pretty as a bluejay in his bright blue coat and white trousers of fine worsted, clean and pressed. A shiny leather cap with a cockade was held in place by a strap beneath his chin.

Proud, the youth looked, too, standing erect and soldierly. Jon didn't blame him. He was a credit to the regular army of the United States government, and he sure looked a lot different from the volunteers who had come up with Pa and beat the English and Indians in the recent war and made possible this garrison in the wilderness.

"Maybe I should be a soldier," Jon thought. "Wouldn't Cindy's eyes pop if she saw me in a rig like that."

There he went again, thinking of Cindy, knowing full well such thoughts could lead to the loss of the freedom he was enjoying now. Another trapper staggered by, grinning foolishly. Freedom? Free to grow old like that, with no kith or kin to care what happened to him? The thought of Ma's brief kiss on his cheek made him glad somebody cared for him.

The soldier grinned and winked, and Jon could see that soldiering at the fort wasn't a very serious business, now the Indian danger was past.

"Your business?" the sentinel's voice was crisp enough.

"Want to talk to Major Whistler," Old Josh said, "'bout some tradin' and trappin'."

"Proceed," the sentinel snapped, and waved them on.

Jon's eyes almost popped at sight of the enclosure. White gravel eliminated the ankle-deep mud of the recent thaw. All about was neat and orderly, a violent contrast to the slatternly look of the area surrounding the palisades. Soldiers walked about, erect and proud in uniforms like the sentinel's, leading Jon to think they must spend their waking hours pressing and polishing.

Two large blockhouses stood diagonally opposite each other, with other buildings in between for officers and soldiers and cook house and stores. Under a double gallery hung a number of leather buckets, painted blue.

"Them's fire buckets," Old Josh said. "Come a fire, and the soldiers grab buckets and run to the river fer water."

Jon chuckled. What a sight that must be, those pretty soldiers running back and forth to the river with water sloshing all over their shiny boots.

"Mornin', Josh," a soldier greeted the old woodranger. "Where'd you get the boy?"

"Caught the varmint in a trap," Old Josh replied, with a chuckle.

"Whyn't you skin him? Weren't his hide any good?"

"Cain't ye see fer yeself what a pore pelt he's got?"

Jon laughed out loud. Oh, it was nice to be with others of his kind, laughing and joshing. Took the raw edge off life, that was for sure.

His eyes focused on a splendidly uniformed man who came out of the officers' quarters. The other soldiers snapped to attention and saluted him as he went by.

"That's Major Whistler," Josh said. "Good mornin', Major."

The major stopped before them, and Jon was awed by his military bearing.

"Good morning, Josh," the major replied pleasantly. "Back to trap and trade, eh?" He jerked his head toward Jon. "Who is your friend?"

Old Josh had suddenly become a model of politeness. "Jonathan Roberts, Major," he replied. "From down Ohio Falls way."

The major held out his hand to Jon and shook hands cordially.

"Luck to you both," he said. "Keep your eyes open. While

the Indians may seem friendly, there are some ready to pounce on unwary travelers and trappers."

On he went across the gravel, leaving Jon to think that he talked just like Ma and Pa and Old Josh. Why, he'd never guess. Just one sorry-looking Potawatami had threatened them, and hunger had likely been the cause of that.

Old Josh crossed the court then, and Jon followed him into a trading post.

"Jest keep still and watch me," the woodranger said. "Ye'll learn the best way to handle these thievin' skunks."

He slapped his peltries down onto the rough counter and untied them. The droopy-lidded, big-nosed man behind the counter brushed them with a scornful hand. "Mighty pore peltries, Josh," he said sourly. "Hardly worth the cost o' shippin' 'em down the river."

Jon bit back his indignation. They weren't the best pelts he'd ever seen, but they weren't the worst either. He watched Old Josh pick up a pair of scissors and then scornfully lay them down.

"Sight better peltries than this junk you're tryin' to buy 'em with," he replied scathingly. He hefted a hatchet, ran a finger over the blade edge. "Steel so soft it'd never take a honin'."

"Best there is, and ye know it," the sutler growled. "Jest come by boat from Marietta."

He gave the bundle of furs a push with a take it or leave it shrug.

Josh snorted and started to retie the thong about the furs. He waved Jon toward the door.

The sutler reconsidered fast, kept pace with them behind the counter. "I'll allow ye a good price fer them furs," he said. "Twice what ye'll get from anybody else."

Old Josh turned, one grizzled eyebrow raised. "How do I

know ye'll give me twice what anybody else will," he said, "till I know what ye'll give?"

"I'll give ye six three-point blankets fer that bundle," the sutler offered.

"Six blankets fer twelve prime beaver pelts?" Old Josh exploded. "Why, Sitkin'll give me at least ten fer 'em. Besides, I ain't anxious fer blankets fer trade goods. Take up too much packroom."

"Blankets is the best kind o' trade goods with Indians up here, and ye know it," the sutler insisted. Then he added, "All right, I'll give ye six three-point blankets and three tommyhawks."

Old Josh kept edging toward the door.

"And three huntin' knives and three pairs o' scissors."

That was his final offer. Old Josh knew it, and he turned and slapped the furs back on the counter. Witheringly, he said, "Ef'n that's the best ye kin do, I'll do ye a good turn and take yer offer."

That trade finished, Jon laid his own beaver skins on the counter and received a like amount of trade goods.

"More o' this," the sutler groaned, "and I'll be a ruined man."

Josh and Jon headed for the door. On the way out Josh had the last word. "More o' this and ye'll be ownin' yer own fur comp'ny."

Outside the old woodranger chuckled. "Best tradin' I ever done with that Yankee skinflint." He slapped the trade goods with a satisfied air. "Squaws are jest crazy about scissors."

They did some trading with Sitkins and two other sutlers at the fort. The same arguments prevailed before satisfactory trades were made. They stopped at the small shop of the silversmith on one of the muddy lanes that ran outside the palisades down toward the riverbank. When they left they had several silver ornaments, such as buckles, armbands, combs, and necklaces.

"This is good stuff, not wuthless trinkets," Old Josh said. "Injuns have a special likin' fer silver."

Jon had been impressed with Josh's shrewdness. The old woodranger had got a much better deal than Jon would have, he knew that.

There was one silver ornament in his pack that would never adorn an Indian squaw. It was a silver comb that he meant to give Cindy. He had been tempted to get one for Ma and one for Emma, but there was no sense loading himself down with too much truck.

➤Chapter-16➤

Josh halted and pointed to a huddle of bark huts set in a copse of bare trees.

"We'll make winter camp here," he said. "A friendly Indian village is the best thing a trader an' trapper kin have around, and if I read my signs right this'n belongs to a bunch of Weas."

Weas! Jon remembered the raccoon roaster and the squaw with the bowl of corn pudding. He was pleased as all get-out. They had been walking steadily for several days since leaving the fort, and he was glad to stop.

A thaw had set in, making it soft and mushy underfoot. It was a good time to set up camp, he thought. Then they'd be ready for business when it turned cold and froze again, as the air told him it soon would.

Several Indian men came out to greet them. With looks and signs and words, they asked the pack-laden newcomers their mission.

"We have come to your village," Josh said solemnly, "to live among our red brothers and hunt and trade with them."

The Indians nodded, pleased. One stepped out and asked boldly, "Firewater?"

Old Josh shook his head. "No firewater," he replied. Then, patting the packs on the horses, he said, "Plenty other things, good things."

"Firewater good," the Indian said, looking disappointed. He barked a few guttural sounds to the others. Their faces clouded momentarily; then they shrugged. "Long walk to fort," the Indian leader said. "We trade."

Old Josh turned to Jon. "That means we're welcome." Then he added softly, "They's plenty others'll give 'em firewater, but I won't. Makes 'em mean and ugly and hard to get along with."

He raised two fingers and spoke to the welcoming group.

"Need two strong bucks," he said.

The spokesman nodded, talked to the others. Two young men stepped forward eagerly.

"Me, Sit-On-Stump," said the first, and indicating his companion, added, "Run-Down-River. We help."

Josh and the two young Indians bargained. Two blankets and a tomahawk for each, plus several silver coins for a winter's help.

"We pay 'em now," the woodranger told Jon.

Jon bridled. "Now? Before they've done anything?"

"It's the way they do things," Old Josh said firmly, getting out his half of the payment. "And it's all right. An Indian makes a bargain, he keeps it. Ye kin most stake yer life on it. Though none of 'em is the hardest workers they is."

The young Indians led them to a good campsite, a hollowed-out place under a bluff some hundred yards back from what Old Josh said they called the Eel River.

"High enough," Josh said, looking around, "so's we kin keep ourselves and the pelts dry, case they's a flood come spring."

Spring! Jon's heart fairly thumped at the sound of the word. Right now he felt a warm breeze on his face, sun on his back, and for one fleeting instant imagined himself in a canoe loaded with prime furs gliding down the Oubache River toward the Ohio. His belt heavy with its pouch of silver and gold coins, he was hurrying to Ma and Pa and the others, even Dave. How he'd welcome their company!

Certainly the company of Old Josh was wearing thin. So were his constant advice, directions, and warnings. Always right, the old man seemed to think he was.

Right? He'd been dead wrong about the Indian danger up here. Only danger, far as Jon could see, was letting the Indians cheat them. Like the old man had done when he'd insisted on paying these young bucks a winter's wage before they lifted a hand. Jon had never yet seen anybody work hard at something he'd already been paid for.

He was right, too. The minute he and Josh started to build their three-sided hut of poles lashed with brush, Sit-On-Stump and Run-Down-River stalked away.

"Why don't they earn their pay by helping us now?" he demanded.

"That's why," Old Josh grunted, and pointed a bony, gnarled finger at the group of squaws and children coming toward them from the village.

"White men do squaw work!" they cried gleefully, and laughed like loons.

Jon scowled and went on with his work. Some boys began playing a game of hoop-and-pole near by.

"I'll show 'em a thing or two," Jon said, and joined them. He soon wished he hadn't. His awkward attempts to throw the pole through the rolling hickory hoop made the boys howl louder than ever.

Jon went back to his work. During the next several days, Sit-On-Stump and Run-Down-River continued to avoid the campsite while he and Old Josh gathered firewood and piled it high about their dwelling.

"I s'pose this is squaw work, too," Jon growled as he threw down another armful of branches.

"It is," Josh replied, "and no brave would catch hisself dead doin' it. The squaws would laugh him right outen camp if he did. But don't git yer back up. Those two bucks'll earn their pay 'fore the winter's over."

"I hope so," Jon said bluntly. "Right now, seems like we paid out good trade goods for nothing."

He felt Old Josh's sharp glance and saw the old man's lips working to hold back a tart reply. Well, it was good enough for the old coot. Let him stew in his own juice a little, too. He was doing enough of it, watching those two Indians strutting around in those new blankets, enjoying things that didn't belong to them.

The whole thing touched a very sore spot, as far as Jon was concerned. How often he had seen Dave doing the same thing.

If only winter would return so they could get on with their business. Right now they were a long way from having a canoe full of peltries. They had done some trading with the Weas, but the Indians, too, were short on furs for the same reason—the weather.

Jon's impatience grew with each passing day.

"Might as well take it easy," Old Josh said one morning as Jon stood disgustedly in the door of the hut, feeding a couple of branches to the feeble fire, which was all the heat they needed in the early chill of the day. "They ain't a thing ye kin do about the weather."

Jon snorted and stalked down to the river. The old man's patience made his skin crawl. Here they were, up north where the supply of fur-bearing animals was limitless, and the old coot was content to putter about the hut and wait.

The old man's unconcern about the way those two bucks were cheating them reminded Jon of Dave, too. And he didn't want to think about that useless brother of his. Right now Dave was probably stuffing himself with Ma's good cooking and warming his feet before a fire that likely was fed with wood Ma and Emma had split and carried in. Jon fairly boiled inside as he walked along the bank toward some marten traps he had set there. Whenever the tension got too bad about the camp he went down to look at them. So far the take had been small.

"Jest ain't the weather fer good trappin'," Old Josh said and continued to wait.

Then, with the speed of a cracking whip, winter returned. It curled bitter winds full of sleet and snow around their hut. The creek froze over with ice thick enough to bear their weight.

Early one morning Sit-On-Stump and Run-Down-River appeared before the hut. With them were several other young Indians.

"Hunt beaver?" Sit-On-Stump directed his question to Jon.

Surprised, Jon looked up from his morning meal of mush.

The Indians, he noticed, carried sticks. On the ends of some were hooks, and on the others were stone chisels.

As Jon quickly rose from the log beside the fire, the Indians jabbered excitedly.

"They say they bin keeping a lookout on a beaver colony not fur away," Old Josh said, grinning. The old man seemed

140

relieved at the appearance of the Indian youths. "Today's a good catch day and they goin' to catch 'em Indian fashion, without traps."

Jon shrugged as he made ready to go with them. What difference how they got the beaver? He had never caught a beaver without a trap, and he wondered how it was done.

"Come," Sit-On-Stump motioned to him when he was ready. He wasn't really a mean-looking Indian, Jon noticed then, as one by one the others fell in behind him and they started off into the forest.

Jon brought up the rear, with Run-Down-River just ahead.

"Why so many?" Jon managed to make himself understood with signs and words. He had never seen more than two trappers together, and there were a dozen in this group.

Run-Down-River grinned at him. "You see," he said pointing one finger at Jon and the other at his own eyes.

It was funny how much could be said in few words, Jon thought.

They came upon a fair-sized creek. The Indians were right about one thing, Jon noted. This was a fine place to catch beaver. A dam had been built by the busy animals, backing the water up into a large pool that spread out into the trees around it. Several high-domed beaver hutches rose in the center of the ice that had formed on its surface.

Run-Down-River halted him at the edge of the pool. Along with several other youths, they watched as the chisel bearers went around the sides of the pond, knocking their chisels against the ice. Sounding out the beavers' holes in the bank, that was plain. The beaver had two retreats in time of danger—his dome-shaped house of twigs and mud with its underwater escape hatch, and his hole in the bank around the pond. Driven from one, he streaked for the other.

Sit-On-Stump let out a cry. The hollow sound of his chisel as it struck the ice told him there was a beaver hole just below. Quickly he chopped a hole in the ice directly above it. Then he motioned to one of the group to come.

Run-Down-River nodded at one of the youths. The youth, carrying a stick with a hook on the end, went over to the hole Sit-On-Stump had made in the ice. He stood above it, with hooked stick ready.

When the beaver streaked from his house to the hole he'd be hooked through the ice. So that was how Indians caught beaver without traps! They were sure smart enough about some things.

Jon became impatient to be called as the chisel bearers tapped and dug holes and yelled for a youth with a hooked stick to come watch each one. But they didn't call him.

Suddenly he realized why: He had no hooked stick. Anger boiled up in him as the meaning of this dawned on him. It hadn't been planned. He wasn't meant to catch any beaver; he had been brought along only to watch!

Then he noticed that Run-Down-River had no hooked stick either, only two clubs. But then they'd divvy up with Run-Down-River. He'd bet a ring-tailed raccoon he'd not get any.

His anger grew; he hadn't been so mad at anybody since the last time he had been mad at Dave! This was the way these thieving redskins earned the trade goods and silver he had given them. Old Josh knew all about Indians and how they kept their bargains, did he? Well, he'd tell that old coot a thing or two when he got back to camp.

Now the pond was ringed with youths standing over ice holes with hooked poles in hand, ready to catch the beaver

142

when they came. Jon felt a club being pressed into his own hand.

"Come," Run-Down-River said, and started out over the ice toward the hutches.

Jon bridled. That crafty Indian wasn't going to put anything over on him. Think he was going out there and pound on those hutches to drive the beaver toward the ice holes for those other Indians to catch? Not him.

"Come!" Run-Down-River yelled again.

Jon refused to move. Folks were always using him to further their own ends; some, like Dave, got away with it. But these Indians he had hired weren't going to do it.

The youths around the pool brandished their hooked sticks at him, yelled, and motioned him toward the center of the pond. Maybe he better go, Jon thought resentfully. He was the only white youth among them, and unarmed at that. A club wouldn't be much protection against those hooks.

He trotted out after Run-Down-River.

Wham! Slap! The heavy clubs hit the thick beaver domes, as he and Run-Down-River belabored them with all their might. Then crack! A cry went up. His club was breaking through.

Jon looked down just in time to see a shadow moving beneath the ice. It was a big beaver leaving his clay home and streaking toward his bank retreat. Little did that beaver know that a hooked stick was poised there, ready to snatch him.

Jon looked up then. He saw the Indian neatly hook the beaver and draw him through the hole in the ice onto the bank, where he killed him with a heavy blow with the stick.

This was better than leaving an animal to die slowly in a trap, Jon thought, and started pounding on another hutch.

Beavers began streaking toward the shore, several at a time. The youths on the bank were kept busy pulling them out and dispatching them. Soon each one had several piled beside him.

Jon was tired. His shoulders ached from pounding with the club. Run-Down-River finally indicated they were through.

Jon stomped back to shore, enviously eyeing the beavers lying all around the pool.

He and Run-Down-River stopped and waited for the others to pick up their catches. Jon didn't doubt that his companion would receive a share when he got back to the village. But what about himself? He had done all that work for nothing.

He was still smarting at the unfairness when he saw the first youth throw his three beaver at Run-Down-River's feet. Jon was surprised to see the next youth throw down his four. He watched, puzzled, as the others did the same.

Then Run-Down-River lined up all the youths, pushing Jon into the line too. Picking up the beaver one by one, Run-Down-River tossed one at the feet of everybody in the line, including Jon.

This went on until all the beaver had been distributed. Each youth wound up with three beaver, except Run-Down-River, who had two. But he only shrugged, picked up his pair, and started off at a trot toward the village.

Jon picked up his three beaver, tossed them over his shoulder, and followed. Not a bad day's catch, he thought with satisfaction. Too bad Old Josh hadn't been along. Still, breaking up those beaver hutches wasn't work for an old man.

➤Chapter-17 ➤

Even before he could see the flicker of the fire in front of the hut he shared with Old Josh, Jon knew something was wrong. He went up over the rise and down on the other side and around an oak tree that stood beside their shelter. The voices coming from the hut grew louder.

"You got firewater!" he heard someone growl angrily.

Jon stopped behind the tree trunk to listen.

"Got no firewater," Old Josh said firmly.

Jon stuck his head around the tree and saw three figures in the shadows cast by the fire. They were Indians, all right. He couldn't see Old Josh and knew he must be in the hut.

"We pay you skins!" One Indian took a threatening step toward the hut brandishing something—Jon couldn't make out what. "Black Cloud and his brothers no cheat like white men do."

Old Josh's voice rang out clearly in the cold air. "No firewater," he repeated. "Never carry it."

"All white traders carry firewater," Black Cloud snarled. "You got. We got furs."

Old Josh stepped out into the glow then, gesticulating. "No

firewater," he said again. "Firewater no good for Indian or white man."

The three Indians took more steps toward Old Josh and the hut. Now Jon saw how they staggered. They were already drunk!

"Never git no closer to a drunk Indian than ye'd git to a snake," Old Josh had warned him.

"You give firewater," Black Cloud roared, "or we burn wigwam and furs."

Jon's heart sank as he saw what Black Cloud carried. It was a stick with rags wrapped around the end, and now the Indian thrust it into the fire to light it.

Jon shut his eyes for an instant, nausea sweeping through him. Burn their furs! A month's work and effort, to say nothing of the days they had spent tramping, would go up in smoke.

"White man think we cheat like white man!" Black Cloud cackled. The sound was silly and meaningless, but the threat to their furs was real.

Jon's eyes popped open, the sight before him searing his consciousness. The flaring flames of the fire and torch etched even deeper the ugly, angry lines in the faces of the drunken Indians. All of them were old, their shoulders hunched beneath their dirty blankets. The black hair of the one called Black Cloud hung stringily from a headband. On one of the others a coonskin cap sat crookedly.

How silly they looked, yet how dangerous. Swaying, they closed in on Old Josh, threatening, "No firewater . . . burn."

Josh didn't flinch.

"Eat plenty," Jon heard him say soothingly, as a mother to a child. Jon saw him point to the frozen carcass of a deer hanging from a nearby limb. "Good meat. Corn cakes. Eat."

146

"No want food," Black Cloud replied belligerently. "Want firewater. You got firewater."

"Got no firewater."

"You lie!" Black Cloud screamed, and lifted the torch. It landed against the side of the hut, fingers of flame reaching hungrily upward.

The other two Indians held their hunting knives threateningly. Even weaving, they looked dangerous and mean. All three cackled as the flames of the torch ignited a piece of bark overlapping the hut. Quickly it flared and leaped farther upward.

"Burn! Burn! Burn white trader hut. Burn furs!"

A feeling of desperation gave Jon strength. He had to do something. He couldn't let those furs go up in smoke. Leaving his beaver on the ground, he raced down the bank and around and up.

Old Josh saw him, but the Indians didn't. Not by the flick of a whisker did Josh betray Jon's presence. Black Cloud's back was toward Jon as he crept up behind him and the other two Indians. They were watching the creeping fire and chortling with glee.

Jon wished he had taken his rifle on the beaver hunt. But Old Josh had told him it would be excess baggage the way Indians hunted beaver. Still, these Indians were so befuddled with firewater that even a rifle wouldn't frighten them. And a shot wouldn't stop the creep of the fire.

His feet made no sound in the snow. Close to Black Cloud Jon made a flying leap and landed on the old Indian's back. With a grunt, Black Cloud fell forward, flat on his face. The other two Indians backed off, grinning stupidly.

Josh moved fast then, grabbed one by the arm and sent the knife spinning. The other Indian reeled away. The old woodranger picked up the knife, then scooped up the torch and heaved it over the fire into the darkness beyond. He threw a handful of snow on the creeping blaze, which sizzled and died out.

Then he and Jon went to work tying the fallen Indians' hands and feet together with strips of deerskin.

"Let 'em sleep," Old Josh said, a touch of compassion in his voice. He looked up suddenly and yelled, "Look out!"

The torch, still alight, came spinning back over their heads, thrown, they knew, by the Indian who had reeled away. Luckily it sailed over the hut and into the darkness beyond.

"The old coot," Josh muttered. "Go out there and git 'im. He'll freeze to death out there by hisself."

The Indian protested feebly as Jon dragged him back like a sack of corn. They tied him up to the other two, now snoring loudly beside the fire.

"They'll bear watchin' tonight," Old Josh said. "Come mornin' and we'll fill 'em up with deer-meat stew and let 'em go. They probably ain't bad Injuns sober."

When morning came the Indians rolled over, blinked, and sat up sheepishly. They asked for the thongs to be cut.

"It is firewater make us do so," Black Cloud said. He made a wry face and accepted the wooden bowl full of stew that Jon held out to him. All three reminded Jon of Old Lightning after a scolding, hangdog and beaten.

They were not Miamis.

"We Delaware," Black Cloud said, drinking the stew in loud noisy gulps, occasionally putting his fingers into it to pull out a piece of meat for chewing. "We sell furs at fort."

"And that's where ye got the firewater?" Old Josh asked. He turned to Jon. "It ain't legal to sell firewater to the Injuns inside the fort, but they's plenty traders outside the palisades

148

that'll do it." Then again to Black Cloud: "Ye said last night ye had furs fer firewater. Where are they?"

Black Cloud looked up, his eyes bleary. "Me say that?"

"Ye sure did."

"Me talk like squaw," he said disgustedly. "Got no fur now." He shook his head sadly. "Trade all for firewater; no get cook pot for squaw. Squaw be mad."

The others looked sad too. "Probably thinking about the things they could have had for their furs," Old Josh commented. "Things that'd last a lot longer than firewater."

When they had eaten their fill the Indians rose, bade Old Josh and Jon goodby, and disappeared into the heavy mists that rose from the cold water of the creek.

Now Old Josh got busy. He didn't have to tell Jon where he was going. Jon had heard Black Cloud say that morning that some Shawnee hunters, not far away, had gone out and returned with a nice catch of beaver and otter.

"Jest hope I git there 'fore some other trader does," the old man said, "or they decide to take 'em to the fort theirselves."

"I hope you do too," Jon said, remembering other trips he and Josh had made, together and separately, to nearby villages. Mostly they had come back with nice bundles of furs and skins, but not always. Twice Josh had arrived in villages to learn that other white traders had beaten him there. Once he had traveled thirty miles through the icy cold only to find another white trader living in the village.

"I'll stay and watch things," Jon promised. He had had his day yesterday when he had gone off with Sit-On-Stump, Run-Down-River, and the others while Josh had stayed behind.

The ways of Indians puzzled Jon. If they made a promise

they kept it, no matter to what lengths they had to go to do it. But stealing was sort of a sport with them, and he didn't want to take a chance having some young bucks take any of the pelts stored in the hut.

Old Josh set off, a pack of trade goods on his back. "Horse no tarnel good in this slippy stuff," he said. Ice had formed a crust on top of a foot of snow and made walking a real chore.

Jon settled himself to a lonely, dreary day. As usual at such times, his thoughts were of home. He never minded cold gray days there. Mostly he'd sit around Ma's neat hearth, whittling, mending harness, shelling corn, or cracking nuts. A fire in a fireplace threw out a sight more warmth and cheer than one before a three-sided hut. Why, just sitting in front of one and staring into the flames could be a pleasant experience, especially if the wind howled around the cabin.

It was howling about the hut now, and biting cold. One never got warm clear through. He sighed now, wishing that for a few hours he could sit around the fireplace at home.

Queer how a body appreciated things so much more when they were far away. At home by the fireplace he'd dreamed of being up north in just such a camp as this, with Old Josh. It would be exciting and adventuresome, he'd thought then, with danger all about.

It was adventuresome, all right—if you could call their experience with the drunken Indians that. It was also dreary and cold at times, and seemed like you'd never know good cheer again.

Deliberately he turned his thoughts to the furs in the hut. His pile was growing steadily, and that was a comfort. It was what he'd left his warm home and come up here for, wasn't it? But the good feeling of accomplishment didn't last long. He was soon moping again.

Chapter Seventeen

"Some trappers come nigh to losing their minds living with loneliness too long," Old Josh had told him. Right now Jon could understand why.

"Reckon I'll go look at my traps," he mumbled aloud. They were set along the creek not far away, and he could keep an eye on the approach to the hut most of the time he was gone.

He shook himself slowly, as he often did now as a gesture against the ever-present cold. His muscles seemed stiff and sore, and no wonder. Even a young man needed a stout puncheon floor between him and the earth if he wanted to ward off rheumatism and such. He picked up his rifle and powder horn and set off down the trail toward the creek.

Some time later he headed back over the same trail with two otters slung over his shoulder. Though chilled, he felt better than when he had left. These were fine prime pelts and would bring a good price when he sold or traded them. Over the crest of a small rise he went, and the hut came into view. He stopped dead in his tracks.

Now how had those three Indians got there without his seeing them? He thought he had had his eye on the approach every minute. But then he knew he hadn't. He had gone around a couple of bends and underneath a bank, searching for his traps. Anyway, there they were, one bending over while the other two watched.

It was Black Cloud and his two friends. Why had they come back? To burn down the hut in revenge for having been tied up all night? The Indians' sense of pride was very great, and to humiliate one was to earn an enemy for life.

There might be another reason they had returned, he quickly decided. They had seen the furs and had come back to steal them. Panic seized Jon in a tight grip. He should have heeded the advice Josh had given him so many times.

"Is different here in the wilderness than it was around the fort," the old woodranger had said. "It was white man agin Indian there. Here it's Indian agin white man, an' they'll show us if they kin that we're the outsiders here. One of us btter stay near our furs all the time."

Josh had stuck around close the day before. Jon should have done the same today.

Such thoughts wouldn't help now, and he knew it. He tried to figure a plan of action. But none came. It was three against one, and the three weren't drunk this morning.

Suddenly Black Cloud barked something that set the other two to laughing. Then they turned and filed off into the forest.

Jon stared, unbelieving. None of them carried anything. The hut wasn't on fire. The stew he had left was still steaming over the fire. What had they been up to?

He raced to the hut and ran around the fire to the spot where the three had been standing. His eye caught some dark objects lying on the snowy ground. Three fine fat otters!

Slumping down beside them, Jon began to laugh silently. With one hand he smoothed the silky fur. The Indians had left the carcasses as payment for their behavior of the night before—and for the kind treatment they'd received, Jon knew.

How wrong could a body be? he thought fiercely. Old Josh and his eternal warnings of dire things that could happen! The old man sure hadn't learned much about the Indians with whom he had lived so long.

➤Chapter-18➤

Hunting and trapping weather held until February. The piles of pelts in the hut grew higher and higher, prime furs and skins that would bring the best prices.

Suddenly a blizzard roared out of the north, cutting and slashing and slinging snow upon snow.

Week followed week when it seemed to Jon they would never see the good brown earth again, when the world seemed a glare of ice-crusted snow that hurt one's eyes to look at.

Animals, unable to find food and having gnawed the bark from trees as high as they could reach, disappeared from the region.

The store of provisions in the bark hut shrank until all that was left was a little corn and bear grease. During a period of several days Jon shot a half-starved squirrel and Josh caught a couple of rabbits in snares, but they barely flavored the thin gruel that was their diet.

The Weas fared no better. Their store of corn from the previous summer was almost gone, as was their supply of bear grease. Sit-On-Stump, Run-Down-River, and the other young braves found no game either, and the few fish they speared through holes in the river ice did not still the pangs of hunger very long.

Faces became gaunt, nerves grew taut, and voices snapped. Like a bunch of hungry hawgs at feeding time, Jon thought grimly, his own insides aching.

In all his thoughts of a winter spent trapping and hunting, he had never pictured a time like this.

"Happens most every winter," Josh told him, " 'ceptin' the mild ones. Lots of Indians starve to death, and so do white men caught in it."

Impatience fed on hunger. Now that he was sure he had enough pelts to sell for the money to pay the entrance fee, Jon itched to be on his way home.

"Ain't likely to git out o' here till the river thaws," Josh said patiently.

"And when will that be?" Jon paced back and forth by the fire.

The old woodranger shrugged. "When the time comes."

Day and night Jon's desire to get back home grew, until it seemed he'd fairly burst with longing. Home . . . hot food for his stomach . . . warmth for his chilled bones . . . the voices of Ma and Pa instead of the guttural gibberish of the Indians.

Even Dave wouldn't faze him anymore. As gray days followed each other Jon wondered if a crack would ever show in the icy armor winter had thrown across the land.

Warm air crept in slowly. Hopes began to rise, only to be dashed again by more bitter cold. Then came a massive thaw —and rain. For three days rain fell steadily, began to seep through the bark hut. Josh and Jon were hard put to keep their furs dry.

"Wet furs ain't worth a hoot at a trading post," Josh said

as they moved the piles about from one dry spot to another.

"Money we get for these we sure earned," Jon said sourly.

"Anything good ye git in life ye earn," Josh replied.

Slowly the ice on the river melted and the water began to rise. For a week it rose, and then other ice began to appear in bigger and bigger chunks.

Old Josh kept a close watch on the river. "Ice breakin' upstream," he said as he and Jon stood on the melting remnants of snow that clung along the bank. "Be right smart of it here come morning."

Jon was elated. "When that's gone it'll mean we'll soon be on our way, won't it?"

"'Less'n somethin' else happens," Old Josh said.

Well, what could? Jon thought irritably. The old man was always busy, it seemed to him, putting out Jon's fires of hope. But that was the old woodranger's way, he'd long since decided.

The gruel was unusually thin that evening. No game had returned, and their meal had been nothing more than melted snow water, with a handful of cornmeal for thickening and a bit of grease for seasoning. It filled none of the crevices in his empty stomach.

Jon thought of his traps across the river, set along a creek that emptied into the larger stream. He hadn't visited them for weeks. He wondered aloud if he'd find maybe a skinny otter in one of them, or any kind of flesh to put in their stew.

Old Josh looked up in alarm. "This ain't no time to try crossin' the river," he said sternly, swallowing a mouthful of gruel. "All them hunks o' ice an' all."

Jon's eyes narrowed. Bossy old coot, treating him like he wasn't dry behind the ears.

"Sit-On-Stump and Run-Down-River came across this afternoon, pretty as you please, jumping from chunk to chunk," he reminded Old Josh sharply.

The old man shook his head. "Them Injun kids larn to do that when they're 'bout knee-high to hummin' birds," he said patiently. "They're light on their feet as falling feathers. Anybody else could get bad hurt that way. Anythin' ye'd find in them traps wouldn't be worth the risk."

The old man went back to his food, slurping noisily as always. Eats like an Indian, Jon thought disgustedly. He scowled and went into the hut. Slumping down on his pile of furs, he pulled the dirty blankets over him and tried to sleep.

Anything he hated, it was being bossed around. His thoughts drifted to the room above the dogtrot at home—mountains of covers, and the distance between them and the cold ground. He could feel Dave wiggle beside him. Dave! Was that why his young brother always sort of bristled when he told him what to do? Did he hate being bossed around, too? On this thought Jon drifted off into a troubled slumber.

It came with a roar in the middle of the night. Jon awoke with a start and sat up. A continuous, thundering crash came from the direction of the river.

Old Josh turned from his brush pallet on the open side of the hut. "Run's choked up," he said. "Likely them ice chunks pilin' up out o' sight."

"Likely higher'n that," Jon said, and tried to go back to sleep. The grinding, crashing sound continued, caused, Jon suspected, by the ice chunks rubbing and tumbling against each other in their haste to be on their way downriver.

He awakened again to see Josh stirring the fire under the

cook pot. The same slop they'd had for supper, Jon thought, only thinner.

He should be up helping the old man, he knew. Old Josh was shaking in the early morning chill, and he moved as though his joints ached. Half warm himself, Jon lay there. He was acting just like Dave again, he thought with astonishment.

Hot, greasy water was about all you could call the meal they ate that morning. Old Josh seemed to read Jon's thoughts.

"Sure, some meat'd taste good in it," he said. "But no sense takin' chances now by trying to cross the river to them traps. It's too close to time fer us to be leavin' these parts fer good."

Jon drained his bowl and said nothing. Just gave Josh a mind-your-own-business look, which he knew was like Dave, too.

Those traps across the river were set a ways back up the little creek. It just might be . . . Jon rose and started toward the river without a backward look.

He was in a surly mood this morning, and he knew it. Best to get away from the old man before his temper triggered. Already the old man's warnings had strengthened his determination to take a look at those traps.

It was drizzling again, and the fog was thick. He bore slightly downriver toward the spot where the stream narrowed. Here the chunks of ice were piled the highest, mixed with tree limbs, rocks, and debris that had been swept along with them.

The run was choked tight. Behind it, upriver as far as he could see in the fog, a mass of ice and debris strained to pass over or around the barrier, but succeeded only in widening it.

Jon stood watching. As the fog lifted he could see that the

piled-up jam reached to the other shore and formed a rumbling bridge across.

"Get across it easy," he thought as he tested an ice cake with the toe of his moccasined foot. The ice cake was jammed tight. "Crossed creeks many a time on rocks slippery as this."

Looking up then, he saw two figures come dancing across the icy bridge and recognized Sit-On-Stump and Run-Down-River. Grinning, they jumped off the last chunk without seeing him and ran up to the village.

They certainly had no trouble. Why should he?

Jon thought of the traps along that creek. If only one of them held a small animal, it would mean meat in the pot and another pelt. Though he didn't need any more pelts, one extra wouldn't hurt.

He started climbing to the top of the piled-up ice chunks. Sticking out here and there were branches, which he grasped to pull himself upward.

Once on top he steadied himself, then took several running steps to the next chunk of ice. The edge tipped as he landed on it, and he teetered to right it. A swift doubt crossed his mind, then vanished as he stepped to the next floating link of his bridge.

On he went, climbing, descending, jumping, sliding, and all the while feeling beneath him the pressure of the jam upstream, pushing, crowding, edging, seeking a breakthrough.

A strange sense of exhilaration filled him. He was going across just as the Indians had, dancing and slipping, but making progress in spite of the hazards.

An ice floe beneath him moved, and he hastily jumped to another, larger, one. His feet went out from under him, and he landed on his backside. But he managed to slither to his feet again and go on, swaying to keep his balance.

A big mass beneath him shifted. Was it the breakthrough? Panic took hold then. All those tons of ice would come down, crushing, grinding. If he should make a misstep and fall between them, they could smash him like an eggshell.

On he ran, swiftly, cautiously. Now he was going downhill . . . his feet hit solid earth. He was over!

He felt weak as the realization of the risk he had taken hit him. Unnecessary risk, as Josh would tell him—if he ever got back to the other side.

Knowing what he had to do gave him strength to do it. With a fresh spurt of speed, he headed for the little creek that emptied into the river.

It seemed months ago that he had set his traps there, hoping to snare beaver or otter or muskrat.

"I hope there's something caught in one of them," he said aloud as he ran. "Something fresh caught, that is, that'll put a taste of meat in the stew we been eating."

He reached the creek and started up its bank. Ice from the river had forced its way up the narrow stream, but not so far as his traps. He was glad of that, for he could never dig beneath the ice to find them if they were covered.

He reached his first trap, set among the exposed roots of a tree that grew half in and half out of the water. The trap was under water now, and it was just as well there was nothing in it.

In the next one, farther up, was the foot of an animal, and he knew the animal had chewed it off rather than stay in the painful grip of the trap's jaws. The third trap yielded a wad of wet fur; another animal had wriggled itself free, though it had left part of its hide behind it.

"Tarnation!" Jon muttered. "Did I come over here for nothin'?"

159

In the next was the limp body of a muskrat, newly caught. Jon let out a shout of joy. There'd be meat in the pot tonight, though he'd seen meat with more fat on it. The fur was good, too.

A grinding sound turned his glance toward the river. Had the breakthrough come? He raced back the way he had come. The ice bridge still held, though like an animal straining at being tied.

Again he found himself on the uneasy floes. Suddenly his footing moved violently, almost plunging him into the surging mass. Righting himself with a mighty effort, he jumped to the rough back of a tree trunk caught momentarily in the ice chunks. When he landed it began to move forward swiftly and more swiftly, until he realized in terror that the jam in the run had broken. The weight of the mass upriver had finally won and was pushing everything in its path downstream with the force of a ramrod in a rifle barrel.

For one wild second Jon felt himself swept along with it. He could be crushed in that mass and ground to pulp as easily as a grain of corn between the stones of a gristmill.

Jon swayed and lurched and almost lost his balance a dozen times. But somehow he leaped from tree trunk to rock to floating tree branch. The swirling, churning water just below was deep and treacherous. Even so, he made some headway across while being swept downstream.

Old Josh's words of warning seared themselves into his brain. Why hadn't he heeded them? Without his furs, the entrance fee would never be paid. And he had been so close to carrying out his plan.

He'd still do it, he determined grimly. He leaped with new-found strength and agility from one floating object to another. By a miracle he stayed upright. A figure was racing down the bank below the Wea village. It was Sit-On-Stump, followed by Run-Down-River. They were waving encouragement to him.

On he went blindly, stepping on something that held him afloat until something else came within leaping distance. He was always mindful that if he fell he'd be brained in seconds by the ice, rocks, and trees that tumbled and cascaded on all sides.

Suddenly he realized he was close to shore. He gave a mighty leap, cleared the floating debris, and landed in shallow water at the edge of the stream.

Strong arms slipped under his shoulders, and Sit-On-Stump and Run-Down-River dragged him up the bank and helped him back to the hut.

Old Josh didn't scold; instead, he said dryly, "Glad ye saved that rat; I kin fix us a real tasty meal outen it."

➤Chapter-19➤

Early one morning, some weeks later, Jon stood in the doorway of the hut. No fire burned before it this morning. Warm and balmy was the air, heavy with the fragrance of spring. Happiness filled him to the brim. Today he and Josh were leaving the Wea village and the hunting and trapping grounds and heading for home!

Jon breathed deeply of the pine-scented air. A smile was broad on his face as he took in the scene before him.

The Eel River was clear of ice and at its normal level, though swift-flowing. Tied to a tree by its bank was the pirogue they had labored on for weeks.

Sit-On-Stump and Run-Down-River had helped girdle the big straight tree, which Josh had picked, and chop it down. They had helped hollow out the log with slow-burning fires and by chipping the charred wood. Together the four of them had shaped it into a fine river craft for carrying Josh and Jon and their furs down to Vincennes on the Wabash River.

Jon's grin broadened even more at the thought. Soon he'd walk into that land office at Jeffersonville and slap down the

$80 needed to register their land against all comers—land grabbers or otherwise.

If somebody, that is, hadn't already done so. That possibility was a small dark cloud hovering over his happiness. Time was important now.

But he wasn't going to think about that this morning. He went into the hut, picked up his last bundle of furs, his rifle, and his tattered deerskin jacket, and headed toward the river for the last time.

Never a backward look did he give the sorry bark hut where he and Josh had lived for so many long days and nights. One didn't look back at something one was happy to be leaving.

Reaching the pirogue, he threw the furs on top of the others stowed in the rear. Old Josh's furs were stowed in the front, and the two of them would sit in the middle.

The iron pot was in the center, too, with a few other items they were taking back with them. "The lighter we travel," Josh said, "the faster we kin go."

"We can't go too fast for me." Jon was jovial. He could humor the old man now. All his dire predictions had come to nothing; everything had turned out fine, and they were on their way home.

And those fine pelts they had received from Sit-On-Stump and Run-Down-River in payment for their horses were stowed with the others now. Everything had gone in their favor and would no doubt keep on until they reached their destination.

"Git in," Old Josh said, gruff as always. "Let's git goin'."

Jon jumped in with alacrity. Sit-On-Stump and Run-Down-River pushed the pirogue into the stream and then

163

watched unemotionally as the pirogue was caught in the current and swiftly pulled away.

Now why did he have a lump in his throat? Jon thought disgustedly as he swallowed hard. Of course, he had grown to like the two Indians. The one thing Old Josh had been right about so far as Indians were concerned was that Sit-On-Stump and Run-Down-River would earn their pay before the winter was over. They certainly had, and without doing any squaw work either.

"Whatcha grinnin' like a chessy cat fer?" Old Josh asked, with more good nature than he generally displayed.

"Thinking of all the squaw work I'll be doing when I get back home," Jon replied with a laugh.

There'd probably be plenty of it to do, work that Dave should have done and hadn't. But this morning he wasn't going to fret about a little thing like that. Sitting down to Ma's good meals again would take the edge off any annoyance he might feel toward Dave from now on.

Jon leaned back, resting against his pile of peltries. Dreamily he eyed the fresh budding world along the riverbank and gazed at puffy white clouds sailing serenely in the clear blue above.

Trees flaunted their new green finery, and bright birds darted among them, uttering sharp joyous cries. The sun shone bright and clear as the pirogue carried them swiftly downriver. Old Josh's hand rested lightly on the pole to guide their craft.

How good the warmth felt on their backs. What a joyous thing it was just being alive, Jon thought happily.

Several miles downriver a group of Indians waved from the left bank and made motions for them to pull in to shore.

"They think we got something to trade," Old Josh said. "And it's too bad, mebbe, we ain't. Likely they got some good furs."

They waved back at the Indians and went on, the angry shouts of the red men coming to them.

"Mebbe it's a good thing we didn't stop," Josh's voice turned grim. "Them Injuns don't exactly sound friendly."

"Gloomin' again," Jon laughed.

The old man looked at him, his faded eyes holding no twinkle. "I know you bin thinkin' I'm too keerful about these Injuns. Mebbe so; but better that way than keerless. Jist don't fergit they's plenty of 'em don't figger white men worth sour apples. It'll take longer'n we got on earth fer some to fergit we took their huntin' grounds from 'em at the Treaty of Greenville."

Jon sobered a little at that, but it didn't last long. On they went to the fork where the Eel and Tippecanoe rivers merged into the Wabash. At the fork there were so many wild turkeys roosting in the trees that the branches shook with the fluttering of their wings while the air was filled with their gobbling.

Jon's mouth watered. "Turkey for stew!" he cried, picking up his rifle from the bottom of the pirogue.

Old Josh slowed the progress of the boat by holding the pole deep down so it scraped the river bottom close to the shore. Jon aimed and fired into the trees. Down through the branches dropped one of the birds. Old Josh steered to shallow water and Jon jumped out, ran to the turkey, and picked it up. It was a fine bird, young and plump.

"It will take a sight of bad cooking to spoil this one." He grinned as he tossed it into the pirogue.

"We'll find a spot along the river somewhere and stop for the night," Old Josh said almost cheerfully. "We'll have it for supper."

Things were going well. They had made good speed down the river; in no time at all they'd be passing Fort Harrison at the high bank the French had named Terre Haute. Then on to Vincennes. Jon could almost feel the pouch of coins hanging from his waist and beating against his thigh. He had traded his last pair of scissors to Sit-On-Stump's mother for the pouch, a fine one made of deerhide with a thong drawstring.

He and Josh had talked it over and decided to sell the pirogue at Vincennes and go by the Buffalo Trace to New Albany.

"Likely we kin buy a couple of horses at Vincennes," Old Josh had said. "Ef'n not, we kin take shanks' mare."

Jon hoped they could buy horses, for he wasn't enthusiastic about walking that far. It would take too long for one thing, and he wanted to get home as fast as possible. But right now he wasn't crossing any bridges until he came to them.

The sun was high overhead when, without stopping, they ate the remaining meat in the iron pot. By the time dusk was settling over the riverbank, they had pulled in to shore and got out.

"I'll take a look around before we build a fire," Josh said cautiously.

"Nothing to fret about around here, is there?" Jon was impatient. He wanted to get that turkey roasting. It would take some time anyway before it was done enough to eat, and the brisk breeze on the water had sharpened his appetite. Seemed like since the spell last winter when rations had been so short, he couldn't get enough to eat.

"We got a big load o' furs in that pirogue," the old wood-ranger reminded him. "They's Indians and whites along this river that'd slit our throats to git their hands on 'em. Ye should know that as well as anybody."

He did know it, Jon thought impatiently. But anybody with a grain of sense could see there was nothing to be wary of around here. The riverbank looked as peaceful as the hearth at home, and with about as many dangers lurking. But then he might as well humor the old man this last time. Lord knew he wouldn't go around him for quite a spell after they got back to New Albany.

He tied the pirogue to the roots of a huge tree left on the bank years ago by floodwaters. Then he stood, rifle ready, while Old Josh disappeared into the underbrush along the bank. The old man meant to climb to the top of the bank, he knew, to see what might be on the other side. Which would be nothing, Jon opined.

A few feet away was a fine overhanging bank that would make a shelter for the night. Fire built there would be hard to see, for it was screened at both ends by tangled bushes. He noted with satisfaction a pile of whitened driftwood not far away that would give them all the fire they needed to roast the turkey.

His mouth was watering for a taste of the juicy meat when he saw Josh come creeping back.

Something was wrong, Jon knew instantly; the old man's manner indicated danger was close by.

"Three Injuns," Josh said softly, "painted and striped fer trouble. Potawatomi, ef'n I ain't mistaken, and they're generally unfriendly and mean. Camped jest over the bank."

The old man paused an instant, then went on. "They got a

prisoner, white boy about fourteen." Old Josh leaned on his rifle, gazed off into the deepening dusk. "I say we oughta try to rescue the lad. What's your opinion?"

Jon gulped, took a deep breath. He knew as well as Josh the risk involved. He wanted to go home. It would be so easy to untie the pirogue, pole it silently back into midstream, and start off downriver and out of danger. Then even if the Indians did discover them, they would be out of danger. But could he leave a boy of his own people in the hands of savages, to be tortured or killed? Old Josh was giving him his final measuring-up.

"We can try." It was Jon's voice that replied, though to him it seemed to come from someone far away. Maybe from God.

Hunching low and making no noise, Jon followed Josh to the top of the hill.

They couldn't fail, he kept telling himself; there was too much at stake: furs, tomahawk claim, the captured boy, their own lives. Jon walked as though disembodied, like two separate entities, one determined, the other praying.

Old Josh stopped at the top of the gentle rise behind the protecting screen of a clump of gnarled, low-growing mulberry trees. Dusk had halted, as it sometimes does on spring nights, seemingly reluctant to lower its curtain of darkness and blot out the day completely. It was still light enough to see the three figures below, hideously painted with stripes and spots of red and blue and green.

Two were making a fire while the other stood silently apart, rifle in hand.

Cold sweat poured over Jon. What if they'd built their own fire before looking around? They'd have been sitting ducks for these three. Old Josh had been right this time.

Then Jon saw the inert figure lying some fifteen feet from the Indians. He knew it was the boy Old Josh meant to set free, even before he made out the matted tow-colored hair on the boy's head. The Indians were paying no attention to their captive. That, at least, was encouraging.

Old Josh squatted down close to the ground, and Jon did the same. They'd wait their chance, and Lord only knew how long that would be. But it seemed only a matter of seconds before Jon's limbs became cramped and sore and the hunger gnawing inside him almost unbearable.

Below, a fire soon leaped and glowed. The Indians cut up the carcass of some animal into chunks, which they stuck onto the ends of sticks to roast. Then they ate it wolfishly, the sentinel coming over to get his share.

The smell of roasting meat made Jon weak with hunger. Why in the name of common sense had they picked this particular spot on the riverbank to camp for the night? Why should they risk their lives for someone they did not even know? Their own lives right now were probably in more danger than the boy's. For many times such boys were brought up by Indian families to replace their own sons who had died.

Likely that was the role this one was intended to play.

Old Josh and his caution. He wasn't being cautious now. Why, they were going out of their way to get into danger. Right now they could go back to the pirogue and within minutes be out of danger.

Old Josh wasn't thinking of his old hide, that was sure; nor of Jon's either. He was thinking about that boy lying there. Well, was that boy any more important than Dave or Uriah? Wouldn't it be better to think of them for a change? Save himself to get back home and look out for them and the rest of the family? Wasn't self-preservation the first law of nature?

The Indians took notice of the boy then, for the first time since Jon had been watching. One brought a stick with some roasted meat on it over to the still figure.

The boy sat up and took the meat. Jon saw his face. Fourteen? He wasn't a day over ten, not much older than Uriah, with his yellow hair standing stiffly above wide, terrified eyes.

Shame swept over Jon. No more than Old Josh could he leave this boy to the mercy of the three savages.

➤Chapter-20➤

"Now!" Old Josh whispered.

The Indians had traveled far and were weary, their manner said. Their bellies full, two of them rolled up in dirty blankets and were soon snoring by the fire. The other, acting as guard, squatted by the blaze and dozed. They were expecting no trouble.

"Cover me," Old Josh said. He pointed to himself and then to the white boy, lying on the ground a good fifteen feet from the fire. The Indians had given him a heavy bearskin to sleep in. It was plain they did not want a sick boy on their hands and were taking no chances with the chill dampness of the riverside night that was settling over their camp.

Josh had his knife out and indicated he was not taking his gun. Jon knew why. It would be awkward cutting the boy's thongs and handling a gun at the same time. Speed was all important, and the old man wanted nothing to hinder him.

His plan was to sneak down, cut the boy loose, and bring him back to the pirogue. With luck, the three of them could be well down the river before the Indians realized what had happened.

Old Josh slipped like a wraith down to the sleeping boy.

171

Jon saw him emerge from the shadows into the faint glow of the fire, saw him slip his knife under the boy's body. He was slitting the thongs that bound the boy's wrists and ankles.

Knowing the dozing guard would be the first to move, Jon kept his rifle sight on him. Old Josh leaned over and whispered into the startled boy's ear. Amazingly enough the boy did not let his surprise show, but sat up dazedly, and then rose to his feet.

The head of the dozing Indian jerked, and Jon's heart sank. Had man or boy made some slight sound to put him on the alert? A mourning dove sent up its weird cry from the river-bank. The Indian's chin dropped to his chest and he dozed off again.

Jon's breath left him in a silent sigh. Old Josh turned and the boy followed, to Jon's dismay, in the solid, clomping walk of one unaccustomed to the ways of the wilderness.

Jon tightened his grip on the rifle and steadied his gaze through the sight. One slight move and the dozing Indian would be a dead Indian.

Then it happened: A twig snapped beneath the foot of the clumsy boy, as loud, it seemed to Jon, as the thunder of a cannon.

In seconds the guard was on his feet, a hair-raising yell escaping his lips. Jon's rifle spoke sharply, and the Indian pitched forward into the fire.

The other two Indians were on their feet before the first hit the ground. With wild yells they grabbed their bows and fitted them with arrows.

Swiftly Jon reloaded his own weapon. But wadding and packing took time, time enough for one of the Indians to take out after Old Josh and the boy.

Josh's voice came out of the darkness, betraying his position. "Take the boy and head for the pirogue," he ordered. Then he picked up his own rifle from the ground where he had left it and turned to face his pursuer.

Jon didn't question Old Josh's order this time. He headed for the pirogue, the boy on his heels. Reaching it, he hastily untied the mooring rope while the boy clambered in.

"Duck," Jon hissed, "so you won't get hit if the Indians fire on us."

The boy ducked, lying on his stomach between piles of furs.

For several agonizing minutes Jon crouched and waited. He could not see what was going on at the top of the rise, but he heard a shot.

Then, suddenly, Old Josh appeared faintly in the distance, walking backward, rifle in hand. Jon sighed in relief. Within minutes they would be on their way downriver, safe and sound when they reached Fort Harrison. From there to Vincennes there would be no Indian danger. White settlers along the river and Fort Knox in between made it a fairly safe stretch and——

Something stumbled against the pirogue and fell on top of them. It was Old Josh, an arrow sticking out of his chest!

"Git goin'," the old man said. "Only one left; dunno where."

Jon straightened up. He was the one who had to get the pirogue into the middle of the river and on its way to Fort Harrison. It was up to him now.

With a strength he didn't know he possessed, he poled the pirogue away from the shore.

Once in midstream, the current took hold and sent the log boat shooting along with it. There was just enough light for Jon to keep the boat in the middle of the stream.

The sky was fairly free of drifting clouds, with stars winking above. Jon remembered that the night before had been moonlight bright, and was thankful. He had to keep their craft away from sandbars and sunken logs, and being able to see what was ahead was of prime importance.

The only sounds were the swish of the water and the old man's labored breathing. That arrow in his chest! If only Jon could stop and do something about it. The boy was worse than useless, his eyes wide with horror, his limbs stiff with fear.

The old man began to mumble. "Won't make it," he said. "Know when I'm done fer."

"Don't talk so!" Jon cried.

"Go home an' stay home," the old man rambled on, half out of his head, Jon knew. "Trappin's no business for the likes of you. I let ye come only to git outen yer blood the hankerin' fer the free life."

Well, it's out good and proper, Jon thought grimly; I've had enough of this sort of thing to last me forever. Once back home I'll stay there, even put up with Dave.

A rasping breath came from Old Josh, searing Jon's consciousness like a red-hot poker. Was the old man right? Was he done for? Jon had never seen anybody die, but he had heard plenty of talk from those who had. The sounds Old Josh was making sounded like those he had heard about.

Sickness crept over him, made him weak. The boy began to cry, dry sobs that tore into his soul. The moon, coming out from behind a big drifting cloud, sent its rays onto the water.

It was a dream, Jon thought; it had to be. He'd awaken soon and find himself in the loft above the Green Tree Tavern with Dave beside him. But the light revealed Josh's blood-soaked jacket as he slumped against the pile of furs. This was no dream; it was grim reality.

The old head rose a bit, and Jon could see the watery old eyes were glazing over.

"He's dyin'!" the boy cried shrilly. "I seen a lot o' dyin' last few days—my Ma an' Pa an' little sister. Them Injuns killed 'em, burned our cabin, and then took me. I wish they'd killed me too!"

The old man's voice could just be heard over the boy's sobbing. It was a hoarse whisper, words forced with his last breath.

"Sell my furs," he said. "Pay off my land. . . . Give it to the Liddicoats. . . ."

The head sank on the bloody chest, and Jon knew he was gone.

"He's dead!" the boy screamed.

Jon nodded. "I know," he said softly, and his own sobs were as dry and racking as the boy's.

All through the night they went downriver, Jon poling the pirogue without really knowing what he was doing. As death does to the living, it sent his thoughts back to better days with Old Josh and made him regret the times he had questioned the old man's wisdom, made light of his warnings. His old friend had been right more often than not, he knew now. Unselfish too. Did one ever really appreciate loyalty and friendship until they were no more?

Well, from now on he'd appreciate what the good Lord had given him so abundantly—parents, loved ones, a home, even neighbors like the John Simonses. In his own way Simons meant well, though it was sometimes hard for Jon to see it. Well, he would manage to make allowances for him from now on.

The boy was asleep, exhausted. Best that way.

Two days later they reached Fort Harrison. Jon and the boy, Jason Burt, were hungry, thirsty, wretched, and sick with horror at having had to travel all that time with a dead man. "He's beginning to smell," Jason had whimpered that morning. And Jon knew they had to go ashore soon.

Men ran from the fort down to the landing to meet the pirogue. They lifted the lifeless body of Old Josh out of the boat and carried it away for burial.

Womenfolk took care of Jon and Jason, fed them and let them sleep. "Don't fret about yer furs," the burly man who lived in the cabin where they stayed soothed the feverish Jon. "I'll see to it nobody touches them."

Three days later, rested and fed, Jon and Jason left Fort Harrison and continued on down the river to Vincennes.

"Ma'll be glad to have you stay with us," Jon told Jason over and over, for the boy kept asking what was going to become of him. "We got a big cabin, and there's room for you in the loft with me and Dave and Uriah."

Blessed thought. But would it be the same as when he had left? It had to be, though fear and doubt began to plague Jon. He had been away a long time and many things could have happened.

Would the Liddicoats still be there with Cindy purring happily in Old Josh's cabin? It would soon be theirs for good; he could hardly wait to tell her. And Pike? What was Pike doing?

Worry chased away the pleasant thought that soon he would be home again. Jon remembered the talk he had heard at Fort Harrison. The petition for statehood for Indiana had been sent to Washington. People now were awaiting word that Congress had passed the act enabling them to elect delegates to a constitutional convention at Corydon.

Law and order would become a reality then. But it also meant the land would be surveyed and put up for sale. Folks with the money could buy what they wanted and have their ownership recorded at the land office. Oh, he had to hurry and pay the entrance fee on their land so their claim to it would be stronger than the mark of a tomahawk.

He sold the furs at Vincennes. His leather pouch was heavy with English and Spanish coins, lots more than enough to pay the entrance fees on both the Robertses and Old Josh's land.

"Where ye headed with that money?" the trader said kindly.

"New Albany."

"River?"

"No. Want to trade my pirogue for a horse, and take the Trace. Know anybody who'd make that trade?"

"Hmmm . . . I will," the trader replied; he knew he could easily sell the pirogue at a profit. He took Jon out to see the horse, not the best in the world, but it would take Jon and Jason to New Albany faster than they could get there on foot.

"I don't advise you to make that trip alone, though," the trader said. "Post rider due to leave here in a day or so. Better ride with him."

It was on the tip of Jon's tongue to tell the man to mind his own business. But he was right, Jon knew. Sometimes, he had learned, it was wise to take the advice of others.

He nodded. "Where'll we wait?"

"There's a fair tavern down the road apiece. Soon's I see the post rider come by I'll tell him about you."

Jon and Jason mounted the horse and rode in the direction the trader had indicated. In no hurry, they ambled along. About a mile down the road they heard the thunder of hoofs approaching them from behind.

Instinctively Jon grabbed his pouch. Hidden beneath a

saddle bag no one could see it. But the storekeeper had seen him put it there. Had he told someone about it? Sent someone to take it away from him?

It was a good two miles more to the tavern, and no cabin that he could see near by. He started to pull off the road and into the woods to hide. But he was too late. Turning, he could tell the rider had seen him. Who was that rider? Somehow the figure on the horse looked very familiar, stocky, with tow-colored hair blowing every which way.

"Jon! Jon!" the cry smote his ears with the force of a thunderbolt. It was—yes, it was Dave!

The horse slid to a stop beside him, and Jon and Dave stared at each other; then both gave whoops of joy and slid to the ground. They hugged each other and pounded each other's shoulders until they were sore.

"The storekeeper said you had just gone," Dave laughed. "And from what he said, I knew it was you, Jon. We been looking for you last couple of weeks. Who's your friend?"

"Jason Burt," Jon said. "He's coming to live with us. What in tunket are you doing in Vincennes?"

"Riding the mail," Dave said proudly. "Regular rider got sick a few weeks ago and I took over for him. Don't fret; I haven't neglected anything at home. Each trip I cut up wood and shoot enough game 'fore I leave to last till I get back. And besides, Ma thought I might meet you here and help you bring all your money home."

It was said only half in jest. Dave gave a low whistle as Jon opened the pouch and let him see the coins. Then he asked where Old Josh was. Jon told him.

"I'm right sorry about that," Dave said soberly. "But the Liddicoats will be happy to get the land and the cabin."

They rode on slowly toward the tavern.

"We'll stay here tonight and go on first thing in the morning," Dave said. "I aimed to stay in Vincennes tonight until I happened into the trading post and heard about you."

Jon gave his brother a curious look. He was talking sense. To start for home now would mean another night on the road, and anybody familiar with the stretch through the forests knew it was better to travel there in the daylight as much as possible. Somehow Jon couldn't remember Dave talking so. He nodded in agreement.

Jon and Dave were almost talked out before they went to sleep that night on the pallets in the loft room of the tavern.

The Liddicoats had had wood and food all winter, Dave told him, with Cindy getting plump as a partridge. Pike had been doing real well taking care of things. He had told Dave he had done what the Larkins had told him to do only because they'd threatened to harm Cindy and Ted and his father if he didn't.

"Pike comes down to see Emma." Dave laughed at the look of astonishment that crossed Jon's face. "And he and Pa talk a lot about that sawmill. Seems Mr. Liddicoat used to work in one 'fore he came out to the Territory."

Dave yawned and went on, "Cain't tell what might happen; might get that sawmill yet."

Dave fell into a deep sleep, but not Jon. He didn't like the talk about Pike and Emma, and that sawmill. He remembered the portmanteau that had belonged to Mr. Jennings. Pike had said he had found that in the road, and he had lied. If a man lies about one thing, he can't be trusted in other things.

Though he would like to think well of Cindy's brother, he was still suspicious.

➤Chapter-21➤

No one was in sight when Jon, Dave, and Jason halted before the door of the Roberts cabin three days later. Dave, as usual, had to have his fun. Cupping his hands about his mouth in the manner of wayfarers, he shouted, "Hallo, there. Lodging for the night?"

A burst of voices came from within the cabin, and the door flew open almost immediately. Ma stood there, staring in disbelief.

"Jon!" she gasped, blinking as though seeing a ghost. "Is it you?"

Dave laughed. "It's him, all right, Ma; our old Injun fighter come back home, with a bag full of money from his furs, too."

Joy brushed Ma's features. Lifting her skirts, she started toward them on the run. Jon slid from the horse, eager to greet her. Ma grabbed him and kissed his cheek, and his own strong arms held her close.

Pa came out, waited patiently. When Ma stepped aside he put an arm about Jon's shoulders and said gently, "It's good to have you back, boy."

Emma was next. She took his hand and squeezed it as

tears filled her eyes. She whispered huskily, "Glad you're home, Jon."

Uriah, who was hugging Jon's knees, looked up and asked, "See any Injuns?"

"A few," Jon replied, smiling, and stooped to hug his young brother. He looked a foot taller, Jon thought.

Straightening up, Jon scrutinized them all hungrily. Gladness swelled in him to see them looking so well. Pa looked better, he thought, than he had seen him look for years. More color in his face, and there was a brightness in his eyes and a new spring in his step. Was it caused by the sawmill in the offing that Dave had mentioned? Had hope, the best of all potions, had this effect?

If that were so, Jon vowed, Pa'd have more of it. He, Jon, would take a hand with that mill and make it more than a hope. And now that the land would soon be theirs legally, he'd give Dave a hand in working it and raising more animals for food and wool for clothing. Such work was a sight better prospect than another winter like the last one, he thought happily.

His eyes took in the stack of firewood by the door and his nostrils sniffed the good cooking smells coming through the doorway. Looked like his brother had done a good job as head of the house while he'd been away, he had to admit.

"Howdy, Jon," Pike greeted him, and only then did Jon notice Cindy's brother. He, too, seemed to have grown a foot this last winter, and filled out until he was no longer the frail-looking lad he had been. Was part of his new strong tallness because he stood straighter and the furtive look was gone?

Now all eyes were on Jason, questioning. A woebegone look was on the boy's face at the sight of all the warmth and joy of loved ones reunited. Hastily Jon lifted Jason down from the horse.

"This is Jason Burt," he announced with a smile, "come to live with us." His look told them not to question him further.

Ma understood. Putting her arm about Jason's shoulders, she said, "I'll bet some vittles would taste good now, wouldn't they, Jason?"

Jason looked into her kindly face. "Yes'm, they would," he said gratefully.

Uriah grinned at him and piped, "You can sleep with me, Jason. I'm Uriah."

That settled, everybody went inside. Looking around, Jon was pleased nothing had been changed there. It was all as he'd remembered it during the months he'd been away. A fire glowed on the hearth, and a steaming kettle hung over it. The big room was clean and scrubbed and orderly, as Ma's house had always been.

Jon knew now he liked it that way.

The noonday meal had been in progress; trenchers half full of food stood on the trestle table. Pones of cornbread were heaped on the pewter platter in the center, and a big squash pie had been cut into wedges ready for sliding onto the trenchers when they emptied.

Ma and Emma bustled about happily, setting out three more trenchers, which they filled from the kettle of stew over the fire. Jon saw the glances exchanged by Pike and Emma, tender looks that conveyed messages needing no words. He wished it were some other boy than Cindy's brother who had turned Emma from a plain girl into a pretty one. He still didn't fully trust Pike, though he knew he had to treat him with civility.

182

Chapter Twenty-One

"How's everything at your house?" he asked as he glanced Pike's way.

Pike grinned at him, and Jon thought of Cindy and the moccasins and silver comb he had brought back for her. He'd take them over as soon as he could, right after he had eaten, as a matter of fact. He could hardly wait to see Cindy's face when he told her the land and the cabin were theirs to keep.

"Everybody's fine," Pike answered. "Even Pa's better, seems like, now he thinks there'll be a sawmill around where he can work." Then he sobered, looking down at his trencher. "Going to be hard moving out of that cabin though. Cindy, 'specially, is going to take it hard. She's learned to like it so, and it's so nice and handy to here."

Jon swallowed hard. He opened his mouth to speak, and saw that Dave was having a hard job keeping quiet. But Pike silenced them both as he said determinedly, "But we're goin' to find a way out, Pa says. He says we'll take up some land of our own, and somehow pay the entrance fee on it. Only trouble is, all the good land close around here's spoke for. . . . But he says we'll find a way." Pike's voice trailed off, his confidence going with it.

Jon's heart went out to him. Now's the time, he thought.

He cleared his throat and said soberly, "Pa says there is no loss without some gain. As Old Josh lay in that boat a'dyin' he said you folks could have his cabin."

Pike's head jerked up and the joy in his eyes was something to behold.

"Then, glory be!" he cried. "We got a cabin and right where we want it. Old Josh took up land, didn't he?"

Jon nodded. "Same's Pa did. Said he didn't know what he'd ever do with it, but he marked it off with a hatchet anyhow."

Pike's fist hit the table a whack. "Then we'll get the money to pay that entrance fee!" he cried. "Somehow we'll get it."

Dave was sitting across the table looking like he would bust wide open any minute. So Jon went on, expansively. "You sure will," he said, "for Old Josh said I should sell his furs and use the money to pay that fee."

Pike's eyes widened as big as hedge apples. Then he stiffened, bit his lip. "You're funnin'," he said softly.

Dave laughed loudly. "Now, Pike, you don't know my brother. He never funs about anything." Dave looked at Jon. "Show him the money in that pouch o' yours," he chuckled. "The half that's his."

"We'll take it over to his cabin right after we eat," Jon said. And everybody knew he had to take the coins over himself so he could be the first to give Pike's sister the good news.

After the noon meal a beaming Pike and Dave and Pa took Jon down to Falling Run Creek where it ran through a corner of their land. They showed him the dam they had started to build with stones and mortar, which Pike and Mr. Roberts and Mr. Liddicoat had been working on that morning. The pool and spill, they said, would power the mill.

"We'll have it ready to go in no time," Jon's father said, "now you're back to help."

Pa was going to be in charge now, Jon could see. He was glad. Did Pa good to be the head of the family again. And he noticed Dave didn't mind having Pa tell him what to do.

Something bothered Jon just the same. "What about the parts we can't build?" he asked anxiously. "Like the blades and such?"

"Scribner boys loaned us money for them," his father said. "They're glad to have a sawmill in the village; make it grow faster if folks can buy their lumber right here. They said we could pay it back as soon as we could."

Jon was surprised and a bit awed at the progress that had been made while he'd been away. He was also anxious to get going, he and Pike. The others understood and didn't hold them more than a few minutes.

He and Pike didn't say much on the way over to Josh's cabin. Each left the other to his thoughts. And for Jon, some of them were sad. He couldn't help thinking of the old wood-ranger who had made it possible for him to be the bearer of good tidings now.

The thump of coins from Old Josh's furs, carefully counted out from his own, made every step a joy mixed with sadness.

But the sadness fled the minute he saw Cindy outside the cabin, carrying a leather bucket of water inside. She let it drop, and the water sloshed over her bare feet. But she didn't notice as she cried, eyes aglow, "Glory be! When did you get back?"

Jon grinned down at her. What a fair sight she was, pink cheeks aglow and wearing, he knew, an old dress of Emma's. As with Pike, good food had filled out the hollows, and se-curity had banished the fear that had once haunted her.

"Bit ago," Jon replied jovially, and then was almost knocked off his feet by Ted, who came charging around the corner of the cabin. The small boy grabbed Jon's knees, just as Uriah had, and asked excitedly, "See any Injuns?"

"A few," Jon replied. And then he greeted Mr. Liddicoat, who came out the door. He looked better, too, almost as much better as his own Pa.

Greetings over, they went inside. Cindy's joy had faded and some of her old anxiety had crept back. Jon knew why, and he set about quickly banishing it forever. He told her and her Pa about Old Josh, and how he had left them the cabin and the money for the entrance fee to the land.

Cindy sat, head down, fingers running creases along the length of the linsey-woolsey dress she wore. Tears glistened on her cheeks. When Jon had given the coins to her astonished father she looked up at him.

"We can't thank you enough," she said softly, "for all you've done for us."

Small and frail she looked again, and Jon hoped right then that he'd always be the one to protect her and bring her good tidings.

"Don't thank me"—he tried to stop the flow of tears as he could never abide to see a woman cry—"thank Old Josh." Then he brought out the moccasins and comb, tied in a piece of deerskin. Quickly he untied them and laid them in Cindy's lap. "You can thank me for these, though."

Cindy sniffed away the tears and giggled. "All right, I will," she said, and rose and brushed his cheek with her lips.

Jon retreated then, happy and blushing furiously.

"I best be going," he said, flustered. "Got a passel of things to do at home."

Main thing was to catch up on the talking that had to be done. Everybody did a noble job of that as the family gathered about the fireplace of the cabin that evening. It was cool enough these nights so that a little warmth was welcome.

Jon was in for another surprise at how well the family had got along without him.

"So you've got the money for the entrance fee," his father said.

Jon nodded. "And a little more'n that," he said with satisfaction.

"Good," his father said. "Then we can take the money

186

your Ma and Dave saved for it and pay back the Scribners' loan."

At his brother's look of shocked disbelief, Dave grinned broadly. He winked at Ma. "We done right well, didn't we, Ma?"

"Now, Dave," his mother admonished, "remember self-praise only goes a little way."

Dave hugged his knees to him in a little-boy gesture of pure delight. "Goes far enough for me," he crowed.

"And none too soon it is for us to square things away," Pa said. "Land around here has all been surveyed and'll be put up for public auction in June. Any that isn't registered will sell to the first who comes forward with money for the entrance fees, whether anybody's living on it or not. It'll go fast now that Indiana is close to being a state."

"How soon'll that be?" Jon asked.

"Middle of summer there'll be a convention in Corydon to draw up our constitution," Pa said proudly. "Jonathan Jennings'll be our first governor, too, looks like."

Ma shook the gourd in which she had put the coins she had laid by. "Till Dave started running the mail while the regular rider was sick, he worked in a store in New Albany," she said. "Made three dollars a week, and we saved every penny of it."

Dave sent Jon an impish look. "Old good-for-nothing, flighty Dave done that," he said, and waited for his mother to cluck at him again.

But she only smiled and said, "I saved a mite of the money I got from folks staying here overnight, too."

In one last burst of pride, Dave said loudly, "There's a bit more'n eighty dollars in that gourd, and we figgered if you didn't make the entrance fee, we would. Now, like Pa says, we can pay back the Scribners and not be beholden to anybody for anything."

Ma hugged the jar and laughed. Jon hadn't seen so much good cheer in many a day. His own spirits soared.

Dave brought out his fiddle then, and everybody sang as he played. It was a heartwarming evening, and even Jason joined in.

It was still dark when Jon and Dave started out next morning. Dave rode Old Lightning; Jon, the horse he had bought in Vincennes.

They hadn't left the Green Tree Tavern far behind when Jon started keeping to the center of the road. He also kept a wary eye out on all the bushes, rocks, and turns along the narrow thoroughfare.

"No need for being so fretful 'tween here and Jeffersonville," Dave said. "Been cabins built up along the road, and besides, since we haven't had any Larkins to worry about, we haven't had any trouble along here, anyhow."

Jon supposed that was true. But he still kept his eyes open, a fact that Dave did not miss. "And Pike is not mixed up with any other hardbats, so don't go thinking what you're thinking about him."

"I'm not so all-fired sold on Pike, even if you and the rest are," Jon said sharply.

"That's because you haven't been around Pike all winter, and we have," Dave replied. "Pike was scared of the Larkins; that's why he did what they told him to."

"He had no more reason to be scared of 'em than you or me, and we didn't join 'em," Jon insisted.

"We didn't live in a three-sided brush hut." Dave was calm and patient with his brother. "Ma and the others could shut the door and bolt it against such trouble, but Cindy and her sick Pa and Ted couldn't. Chet and Jed kept telling Pike they'd do his folks in if he didn't do what they said.

"And that satchel that belonged to Mr. Jennings," Dave took the words right out of Jon's mouth. "Pike said he found it in the road after Mr. Jennings had thrown it at Chet, and that Chet had left it there when he found there was nothing in it but fancy shirts."

Fear and suspicion left Jon then, to be replaced by a feeling strange to him: respect for Dave and his thoughts and ideas. Why, that brother of his had good sense, after all.

"Like Pike, don't you?" Jon asked him.

"Sure do," Dave answered warmly. "Been around him a lot this past winter, and I know they don't come any better."

They rode the rest of the six miles between New Albany and Jeffersonville in silence. Once inside the small building that housed the land office, Jon handed over his money and received a paper stating he had made the first payment on their land. It was a tomahawk claim no longer.

On the way back they ate the food Ma and Emma had fixed for them, and Dave began to sing. Jon, feeling as light-hearted as a songbird, joined in.

Dave sent him an amused look. "It ain't like you, Jon, to sing and take on so."

"Maybe now I feel like singing and hollering," was Jon's reply, "now I earned the money for that entrance fee and paid it."

Dave gave his brother a searching look; then he snorted, "You done that all by yourself, didn't you? Me and Ma and Emma didn't do a thing so's you could go up north with Old Josh, like you wanted to do more'n anything."

Jon was taken aback. "You don't need to get your back up," he said "Course you helped, but . . ."

"It was still you that done it all . . . just like it was me that put all that money in Ma's gourd, with no help from her or anybody!"

Jon's jaw dropped. Never had he heard such plain talk from Dave. Here, he knew now, was somebody to be reckoned with.

The realization gave him pleasure, too. Why, with Dave near grown and Pa well now, the Roberts menfolk could really do all the things they had dreamed of doing here on the frontier. They could pay off their land in the next few years and live like Ma had a right to expect.

Jon spoke up admiringly: "You did a bit of growing up last winter, Dave."

Dave started to laugh. "Now, it's right big of you to say that, Jon." Impishly, he added, "And I might say you did a mite of growing up yourself, brother."